SEARCHING FOR SUNSHINE

by Ben M. Baglio

Cover art by Andrew Beckett
Interior art by Meg Aubrey

SCHOLASTIC INC.

New York   Toronto   London   Auckland   Sydney
Mexico City   New Delhi   Hong Kong   Buenos Aires

Special thanks to Liss Norton

ISBN 0-439-79249-5

Text copyright © 2005 by Working Partners Limited.
Illustrations copyright © 2005 by Scholastic Inc.

12 11 10 9 8 7 6 5 4 3 2   5 6 7 8 9 10/0

Printed in the U.S.A.
First Scholastic printing, October 2005

Chapter One

The package was waiting for Andi Talbot when she got home from school. "It's from Dad!" she whooped, recognizing his writing on the large brown envelope.

Buddy, Andi's Jack Russell terrier, came bounding out of the living room at the sound of her voice.

Andi bent down to pat him. "Hey, Bud. Have you been good?"

"Good as gold, apart from getting under my feet all day," Judy Talbot joked, appearing in the kitchen doorway. "Sometimes I wonder why I take days off. Looking after Bud is far more tiring than office work."

Andi laughed. She knew her mom loved Buddy almost as much as she did.

"What's your dad sent you?" Mrs. Talbot asked.

Andi tore open the package. It contained a letter, a packet of seeds, and a large white envelope. She

1

scanned the letter quickly. "Dad's sent a present early because he's going to be away on my birthday." She sighed. "I haven't seen him in ages. I wish he didn't have to work so hard."

Mrs. Talbot gave Andi a hug. "He'll come and see you as soon as he has a vacation, I'm sure. What else does he say?"

Andi turned to the letter again. "These are for you." She handed the seeds to her mom. "Lemon balm. Dad says you should grow them by the back door so you'll brush against them every time you go outside. He says you'll like the lemony smell." Andi's parents had been divorced for three years now, but Andi loved the fact they still got along well.

"That's nice of him," Mrs. Talbot said. "What's in the envelope?"

Andi tore it open. It contained a brochure for the Hollow Creek Riding Center, and there was a book of twelve vouchers for riding lessons. Hollow Creek was located just outside Orchard Park, the suburb of Seattle where Andi and her mom lived. "Awesome!" Andi shouted. Her dad had taken her trail riding in the Rockies during the summer vacation and she'd had a wonderful time. "Now I can really learn to ride!" she announced with a grin.

The oven timer beeped then, and Mrs. Talbot hurried into the kitchen.

Andi picked up Buddy's favorite squeaky rubber bone and tossed it along the hall. "Fetch, Bud!"

Buddy bounded after it. He snatched it up, came racing back to Andi, and dropped it at her feet.

"Good boy." Andi ruffled his ears then threw the bone again. As Buddy charged away, she sat down on the stairs and flipped through the brochure. There were a bunch of photos of cute ponies being ridden along trails, and there was a picture of a big outdoor arena, too. "These stables look incredible!" she called to her mom. "Can I start this Saturday morning?"

Her mom came out of the kitchen. "Well, I don't know."

"Why not?"

"You always take Buddy for his long run on Saturdays. You know our deal. I come home from work at lunch during the week to give him walks, but he's your responsibility on weekends."

"I'll only be riding for an hour or so!" Andi couldn't understand why her mom was making such a big deal out of it. Was she expected to stay home every Saturday just because she had a dog?

"But getting there and back is going to take time," Mrs. Talbot said. "You know I shop on Saturday mornings."

"We can buy groceries anytime!" Andi hated arguing, but her mom knew she'd wanted to learn to ride seriously ever since her trail-riding vacation.

Mrs. Talbot sighed. "Maybe we can sort something out. How about if you take Buddy for a shorter walk on Saturday afternoons, after you've ridden, and a really long one on Sundays?"

"Whatever!" Andi snapped, still annoyed. "I can find a bus that goes near the stables if shopping's such a big deal. And I'll take Buddy with me." She stomped upstairs with the little Jack Russell trotting behind her.

"Andi, I don't like your tone! You're not acting like someone who deserves riding lessons!" her mom called after her.

Andi didn't reply. She went into her mom's study and slammed the door. She'd been thrilled at the thought of learning to ride, but her mom's reaction had been like a cold shower. "You won't mind if I go riding, will you, Bud?" she asked, sitting down at the computer.

Buddy flopped down across her feet with a contented sigh.

Andi stroked his ears, then switched on the computer. "I'll e-mail Dad, to thank him for the present." She paused, thinking about the fight between her and her mom. "And then I guess I'd better go downstairs and apologize."

"Guess what!" Andi yelled, racing across the schoolyard to join her best friends, Natalie and Tristan, the next morning.

"Another case?" Natalie asked excitedly.

"Excellent!" Tristan said. He flung down his backpack with a groan. "This thing weighs a ton. Ms. Ashworthy's gone homework crazy!"

"Good for you, Tris," Natalie said. "You don't want your brain seizing up." She turned to Andi, her blue eyes shining. "So tell us all about it. Are the Pet Finders in business again?"

Andi, Natalie, and Tristan had organized the Pet Finders Club to help track down lost animals. They'd met up when Andi had lost Buddy just after moving to Orchard Park from Florida. They made a great team and had already tracked down a bunch of missing pets.

"It's not a new case," Andi said. "My dad bought me horseback riding lessons."

Natalie wrinkled her nose. *"Riding lessons?"*

"I loved trail riding in the Rockies!" Andi explained. "My dad took me last summer."

Natalie tossed back her blond hair. "Riding's okay, I guess. I rode while I was at camp."

"It's way too dangerous," Tristan said. "People fall off horses and break their arms and stuff."

Andi raised her eyebrows at him. "Not like skateboarding, then," she said with mock seriousness. "Nobody *ever* gets hurt falling off a skateboard." Tristan spent half his life glued to a skateboard, and the other half coming unglued in a pretty spectacular way. Just now, he had a bandage on his chin and one on each hand, souvenirs from his most recent falls. Andi was pretty sure he had skinned knees and elbows, too, but they were hidden by his jacket and jeans.

"It's hardly the same thing," Tristan began. Before he could say anything else, the bell rang for the start of school.

Natalie linked arms with Andi. "Come on, Annie Oakley. Hitch up your horse and let's get into school."

"I can't wait to get on a pony again!" Andi exclaimed for the millionth time Saturday morning, as they headed for the riding stables. Her mom had agreed to let her go riding on Saturdays after Andi had apologized for being rude and promised she'd make sure Buddy got plenty of attention in the afternoon.

Buddy was standing on Andi's lap, gazing out of the window. He seemed to sense Andi's excitement because every few seconds he gave a little high-pitched bark.

Andi hugged him. "Is it much farther, Mom?"

"I think we're almost there." Mrs. Talbot met her eyes in the rearview mirror. "Poor Buddy, he thinks he's going for a walk."

"I'll take you for a walk this afternoon, Bud," Andi told him, rubbing his tummy.

Buddy licked her nose.

They were out in the countryside now, with fields on either side of the road. The trees were almost bare; only a handful of yellow leaves still clung to the branches. The mountains loomed up ahead, their craggy tops hidden by low clouds. Andi's excitement grew as they drove on. The mountains were the things she liked best about living in Seattle — they were so different from anything she'd seen in Florida.

She pointed ahead suddenly. "Look!" A wooden sign standing by the roadside read HOLLOW CREEK RIDING CENTER. It was decorated with pictures of horses and a black arrow that pointed them to the right.

Mrs. Talbot turned onto a stony drive that sloped steeply uphill. Ahead, Andi could see a collection of old, red-roofed buildings. Beyond the buildings, sloping grassy fields stretched away to a pine forest. In one of the fields, a herd of red-and-white cows were grazing; in another, a huddle of ponies stood close together. Farther off still, the mountains rose up and up until they met the sky.

Andi's mom drove into the yard and parked near an L-shaped stable block. Andi watched eagerly as two teenage girls came out of a stable leading a brown pony. *That'll be me soon*, she thought with a thrill of excitement. Another girl appeared carrying a saddle. "Hang on, you two!" she called, hurrying after her friends.

On the far side of the yard stood a single-story house and a large barn. A woman about Mrs. Talbot's age, with tousled black hair and wearing a battered windbreaker, came out of one of the stables. "Hi there!" she called. "Welcome to Hollow Creek. I'm Mrs. O'Connor, the owner."

"Hi! I have a voucher for a riding lesson."

Mrs. O'Connor smiled. "You must be Andi Talbot."

"Yep!" Buddy jumped down from the car, his tail wagging enthusiastically.

"Well, he's a cute little ball of energy!" Mrs. O'Connor bent down to rub Buddy's ears. "But keep him on his leash, okay? We have livestock here."

"Sure." Tightening her grip on Buddy's leash, Andi

looked around. She counted fifteen stable doors. Most of them were closed, but a dappled gray horse was looking out of the nearest stable. Andi went over to pet him. "Aren't you a beauty?" she murmured, rubbing his nose.

The horse nuzzled her hand as though he hoped she might have a treat.

"Let's go put Andi's lessons on the calendar, Judy," said Mrs. O'Connor.

"I won't be long, Andi!" Mrs. Talbot called.

Andi smiled over her shoulder. "Bud and I will go explore." She said good-bye to the horse, then headed for the barn. Inside, she was surprised to find a herd of small black-and-white goats. "Hey, these don't look much like horses," she laughed.

Buddy scampered up to the goats' pen, pulling Andi behind him. "They're goats, Bud," she told him. "I guess you've never seen one before."

A young goat was leaning against the fence. It jumped away when Buddy appeared, then tiptoed back to stare curiously at him through the rails.

"It's okay." Andi reached over the fence to pet the goat. "He won't hurt you." To her surprise, the goat's fur was soft and silky. She'd expected it to feel much coarser.

The goat reared up on its hind legs then, and rested its front hooves on the fence. "Aren't you pretty?" Andi said. The goat turned its head and tried to nibble her sleeve. Laughing, Andi drew her hand back. The goat bleated.

The sound must have startled Buddy because he began to bark. The goat skittered away from the fence.

"Be quiet, Buddy!" Andi scolded. She scooped him up and carried him out of the barn.

A dark-haired girl about eighteen years old was leading two ponies across the yard. One was a small, shaggy brown mare, the other a sturdy chestnut with three white socks. A blond, round-faced boy about ten, and a girl a couple of years younger, who looked so much like him that she had to be his sister, watched eagerly.

"I hope the little one's mine!" the girl exclaimed. "She's so cute!"

Andi crossed the yard, wondering where her mom had gone. Suddenly, she spotted a white duck with a yellow bill waddling along between the barn and the end of the stable.

Buddy spotted the duck, too. He wriggled furiously in Andi's arms.

"Hold still, Bud!" Andi scolded.

Buddy squirmed even more. Andi couldn't hold him a second longer. He wriggled free, dropped to the ground, and charged away, barking loudly. Andi stomped on the end of his leash, but it slid out from under her foot.

"Buddy!" she yelled, racing after him. "Come back!"

Buddy disappeared around the corner and Andi heard an explosion of quacks. She burst out from between the buildings in time to see him leaping into a duck pond. Muddy water flew up around him, and the ducks scattered in all directions.

Andi was horrified. "Buddy! Come here!"

He ignored her and stayed in the pond, barking madly, as though he were playing the best game ever.

"Buddy!" Andi yelled again.

Suddenly, a dark-haired boy came running around the side of the barn. "What on earth do you think you're doing?" he demanded, splashing into the pond. He caught Buddy by the collar and hauled him out. "Letting a dog loose! Are you out of your mind?"

"I'm sorry," Andi began. "He — "

The boy didn't let her finish. "You shouldn't be in charge of a dog. You obviously don't know a thing about animals!"

Andi was furious. "For your information, I know a lot about animals!"

"Oh, yeah? Well, it doesn't look like it from where I'm standing." The boy thrust Buddy's leash into Andi's hand and stomped away.

Chapter Two

Andi glared after the boy. She was about to charge after him and tell him exactly what she thought of him, when Buddy jumped up and planted his muddy paws on her jeans. "Oh, Buddy!" she wailed.

She pushed him down and held him on a short leash. Then, crouching beside him, she pulled up a handful of long grass and began to rub at the mud that coated his legs and tummy.

Buddy licked her nose.

"You're not getting away with this that easily. I can't believe you embarrassed me like that, chasing those poor ducks!"

The handful of grass was soon caked in mud and Buddy looked no cleaner than before. Andi threw it down. "Let's get you back to the car." She hoped she wouldn't see the boy again as she led Buddy back through the yard. To her relief there was no sign of him.

Keeping a tight grip on Buddy's leash, she crossed the yard quickly, trying not to look at any of the other riders. Buddy was so filthy they'd probably all be staring. Reaching the car, she opened the trunk and took out the old towel she kept there. Buddy seemed to have a homing instinct for muddy puddles, and Andi regularly had to rub him down when they'd been for a long walk.

She was halfway through drying him when her mom came out of Mrs. O'Connor's office. "All done!" she said. "And your lesson . . ." She trailed off. "Oh, Andi. What's Buddy been up to now?"

Andi told her about the duck pond without mentioning the dark-haired boy. She felt a bit guilty, because she should have known better than to let Buddy chase the ducks.

Mrs. Talbot sighed. "I knew something like this would happen. Buddy's used to running off his energy with a long walk on Saturday mornings."

Andi didn't want to hear this all over again. She heard horse's hooves behind her and glanced around. An older dark-haired girl was walking toward her leading a buckskin pony. "Hi, are you Andi?"

"That's right."

The girl smiled. "I'm Shona, your group leader. This is Sunshine, the pony you'll be riding."

Andi looked at the copper-colored mare. She had a pale gray mane and tail and huge, friendly brown eyes. "She's definitely the brightest sunshine I've seen in Seattle so far!" she joked.

Shona laughed. "Do you want to come and tack her up?"

"Yes!" Andi had loved putting Clancy's saddle and bridle on when she'd been riding in the Rockies. It made her feel like a *real* rider.

As Shona led the pony forward, Andi noticed that there was a dark streak in her tail. "That's weird, isn't it?" she asked.

"Well, I've never seen another buckskin with a tail like it. But it's pretty, don't you think?"

"Oh, yeah." Andi quickly wiped the last trace of mud from Buddy's coat. She opened the car door and he jumped in. "See you later, Bud," she said, leaning in to pet him. He looked up at her unhappily and began to whine. "It's okay, boy. I'll only be gone an hour."

She shut the car door and Buddy flopped down on the seat with his head on his paws. Andi felt a stab of guilt and turned away quickly. *Buddy will enjoy going to the garden center with Mom*, she told herself. He loved trotting along the aisles and sniffing all the plants.

"Enjoy your ride," Mrs. Talbot said.

"I will! See you in an hour." Andi took the pony's reins, suddenly feeling a little nervous.

"Sunshine will take care of you," Shona said, as if she'd noticed Andi's expression change. "She's really good-natured. You've already done some riding, anyway, right?"

"Yes, I went trail riding in the Rockies with my dad during summer vacation."

Shona's smile broadened. "Lucky you! I'd love to do that. Come on and meet your group." She strode across the yard toward the blond boy and girl. Four ponies and a horse were tied to a rail, and the girl was hugging a shaggy pony as though she didn't ever want to let go. Another boy, thin and wiry and about eleven years old, was tightening the girth on a sorrel pony. The pony's light chestnut coat was flecked with white that looked a bit like snowflakes.

Andi kept pace with Shona, and Sunshine walked willingly beside her.

"We're going on a trail ride today so I can assess you before we ride in the school," Shona explained. "Trail riding is a really great way to meet the horses, and there's all this beautiful scenery, too."

Andi gazed up at the mountains. "You can say that again!"

"Meet Andi, everyone," Shona said as they joined the rest of the group. "This is Tim and Helen." She waved a hand toward the blond kids. "Helen's riding Scrumpy and Tim's on Bonnie. And this is Darryl and Chipper." She patted the sorrel pony. "How are you doing with that girth?" She checked the strap that held Chipper's saddle in place. "Great! You've done a good job."

Darryl smiled. "Thanks."

"Now, you need to grab Sunshine's saddle, Andi. Tie her to the rail first."

Andi looped the reins around the rail and tied them securely. She didn't want her pony running off — trying to catch Buddy had been bad enough!

"The tack room's over there." Shona pointed. "The saddle's on your right as you go inside. You'll see Sunshine's name on the shelf."

Andi found the saddle easily and lifted it down. By the time she got back to the group, another girl had joined them. She was very tall, a good head taller than Andi — though she didn't look much older. Her fair hair was

cropped short. She was wearing a pair of jodhpurs. The close-fitting riding trousers were so well worn that the seat and the inside of the thighs were shiny. The girl was stroking Sunshine.

"Hi," Andi said. "I'm Andi."

"I'm Sara." The girl glanced briefly at Andi then turned back to Sunshine.

Andi placed the saddle on Sunshine's back.

"What are you doing?" Sara asked sharply. "I want to ride this pony."

Andi looked at her in surprise. "But Shona said . . ."

Sara didn't let her finish. "I mean, she's so cute," she added, sounding a bit more friendly.

"Actually, Sara, you're on Tilly," Shona said. "You're a more experienced rider than Andi, and Tilly isn't suitable for a novice."

Tilly was tied to the other end of the rail. She was the best-looking of all the ponies, reddish-brown with a black mane and tail. Sunshine was adorable, but Tilly was even more striking. Andi was sure Sara would be happy to ride her.

Sara hardly glanced at Tilly. "Please let me ride Sunshine," she begged.

Shona looked surprised. "I'm sorry, but Sunshine really is much more suitable for Andi. Maybe you can ride her another time." She lifted Sunshine's saddle flap and examined the buckles that held the girth in place. "Good job, Andi," she said. "Take a look, everyone. Andi's done a great job with this girth."

The other riders crowded around.

"She's cinched it tight," Shona went on, "but with just enough room to slip her hand underneath and smooth down Sunshine's hair behind her front leg. Any tighter and Sunshine wouldn't be able to breathe or move comfortably. Any looser and the saddle would slip." She looked up and smiled at everyone. "Okay. Let's mount up! Does anyone need a hand? Helen?"

"I can manage, thanks," Helen replied. She placed one foot in the stirrup and hauled herself up. Shona guided her other foot into the second stirrup, and the little girl sat up straight, grinning with delight.

Andi unhitched Sunshine from the rail and swung herself into the saddle. It felt good to be on a horse again, and she tried to remember all the things she'd learned on her vacation. She sat deep in the Western-style saddle, letting her legs hang comfortably, and held the reins lightly in her right hand.

Sara finished saddling Tilly and mounted without looking at Andi or Sunshine.

Shona climbed onto her long-legged horse. The

horse's reddish brown coat was spotted with gray, and she had a black mane and tail. "Pretty horse, Shona," Andi said. "What do you call that color?"

"Harley is a roan. It's my favorite color." Shona patted Harley's neck. "Now, let's go!" She led the way around the side of the stables, and Andi and the others followed.

They skirted the edge of the field where the cows were grazing, keeping to a path that ran next to a river. The paddock with the other ponies in it sloped uphill, and the gate at the far end led right into the forest that covered the mountainside. Andi felt a tingle of excitement as they rode toward the pine trees, the ponies' hooves thudding softly on the grass.

Shona rode in front with Helen. The little girl was chatting about how much she loved ponies and how she wanted one of her own someday. Darryl and Tim rode side by side, not talking much. Sara rode behind them. Andi stopped to shut the paddock gate and fell a little behind. She gave Sunshine a gentle kick and the pony began to trot. Andi leaned forward to pat her neck as she rose and fell in time to Sunshine's stride. She was glad she hadn't forgotten how to post to the trot, since her vacation seemed like ages ago.

As she came alongside Sara, the girl looked around.

"It's great out here, isn't it?" Andi said eagerly, reining Sunshine to a walk.

"Yeah, I guess."

"Have you done a lot of riding?" Andi persisted, trying to get a conversation going.

"Yeah, a lot." Sara didn't look up at her; she was staring at Sunshine's flank instead.

"Is there something wrong with my stirrups?" Andi asked.

Sara looked surprised. "No, why?"

"I thought you were looking at them just now. Maybe I'm not sitting right, is that it?" Andi sat straighter in the saddle.

"No, you're fine," Sara said. They rode on in silence for a while.

Andi noticed that Sara kept shooting sideways glances at her. "Am I holding the reins right? The group leader from my trip in the Rockies said ponies should have a bit of slack in Western riding. Am I giving Sunshine enough? Or too much, maybe?"

Sara shrugged. "About right, I'd say."

Andi began to feel uncomfortable. "So, have you been to Hollow Creek Riding Center before?" she asked.

"No."

Andi wondered if Sara was jealous of her because

she was riding Sunshine. But Shona had already said she could ask to ride Sunshine next time.

When they reached the edge of the woods, Shona halted. She turned around in her saddle. "Good job, everyone. Great riding so far! Tim, don't forget to keep your reins loose — you don't need to keep a contact on the bit all the time."

They entered the woods in single file because the trail was so narrow. Andi rode at the back. The path was thick with fallen pine needles and the ponies' hooves made almost no sound. A few birds sang and once a squirrel chattered at them as they passed.

Rounding a bend in the path, they came upon a fallen tree, its trunk green with moss. Tilly shied away from it, snorting. Sara sat very still and closed her legs against the pony's flanks. After a couple of steps, Tilly calmed down.

"Wow, you're a really good rider!" Andi said admiringly.

Sara didn't reply. Andi followed, more puzzled than ever.

They came out of the woods onto a stretch of grass dotted with spindly trees. On the far side lay a massive boulder. Andi wondered if it had broken away from the mountain years ago and bounced and rolled its way down before coming to a stop here.

Ahead of them, a river glittered in the fall sunshine.

"This river gave Hollow Creek its name," Shona explained. "It vanishes underground in a cave higher up the mountain, near those old buildings." She pointed out a cluster of ramshackle barns that clung to the slope about a quarter of a mile above them. The buildings were precariously perched on the very edge of a steep cliff. Even from this distance, Andi could see that they were in ruins, with holes in the roofs and walls.

"What are they?" Darryl asked.

"That's Hollow Creek Farm. It was built by Polish immigrants about thirty years ago, but the floods have eroded the ground and the buildings are too dangerous to use now. If any more ground falls away, they'll go with it. The road to the farm is dangerous, too, especially in bad weather. It's really steep and rocky." Shona shivered. "I always think the place looks haunted."

Andi stayed where she was for a few moments, looking up at the old farm. Living in such an isolated place would have been pretty scary, even if the buildings hadn't been hanging on the edge of a cliff. Shona was right: It *did* look haunted, like an old movie set. Andi could just imagine the ghost of a farmer stumbling around on a stormy winter night, searching desperately for the possessions he had lost in the flood. . . .

She grinned, realizing that was the sort of thing Tristan might say, as she urged Sunshine into a trot to catch up with the others.

She soon reached the enormous boulder. As she trotted past, a brown speckled snake suddenly slithered down from it. Sunshine leaped back with a shrill whinny of fright!

"Whoa, girl!" Andi cried. She tried to shorten the reins, but Sunshine jerked her head, yanking them from Andi's hands.

A moment later, she was bolting across the grass at top speed!

Chapter Three

Terrified, Andi grabbed for the reins and pulled hard. But Sunshine was thoroughly spooked and didn't break her stride at all as she galloped uphill. Andi felt herself slipping sideways in the saddle and buried her hands in Sunshine's mane. She flashed past Shona and the other riders, catching only a glimpse of their shocked faces.

"Hang on, Andi! I'm coming!" Shona yelled.

Sunshine streaked full tilt toward the river. Still clinging on for dear life, Andi prayed the pony would stop once she reached the water. But to her dismay, Sunshine charged through the shallows, her hooves cracking hard over the pebbles. She sprang out on the other side and galloped on. Andi shut her eyes, feeling dizzy with fear.

Suddenly, she heard different hoofbeats. Cautiously, she opened her eyes. A pale horse was almost level with her. The rider leaned out of the saddle and caught Sunshine's reins. "Easy, girl!"

Then Sunshine slowed down gradually as the reins went taut — first to a canter, then to a trot, and finally to a walk.

Shakily, Andi straightened up and turned to her rescuer, wanting to thank him. She opened her mouth, but nothing came out. It was the boy from the Riding Center who had shouted at her earlier.

"Now what were you doing? Seems like you need to keep better control of your pony," he grumbled.

"It wasn't my fault!" Andi replied indignantly. "A snake scared her."

"It was so your fault!"

Shona cantered up, her face pale. "Andi, are you all right?"

"Yes, thanks. Just a little shaky."

"Thank goodness you managed to hold on. And that you were nearby, Neil. I don't know what would have happened if you hadn't stopped Sunshine when you did."

Andi patted Sunshine's slippery neck. She didn't trust herself to say anything more. She certainly wasn't about to act like Neil was any kind of hero. The pony was calmer now. She'd stopped trembling and was reaching up to touch noses with the boy's horse. Andi noticed that it was a palomino, a pale tan horse with a silver mane and tail.

"Andi, this is Neil O'Connor," Shona added. "He's Mrs. O'Connor's son. And, Neil, this is Andi Talbot."

Neil tightened his grip on Sunshine's reins. "I guess we'd better get you back to the group. Go ahead, Shona. I'll take care of Andi."

"I don't need taking care of, thank you very much," Andi snapped when Shona had gone.

Neil grinned unexpectedly, his teeth white against his tanned skin. "That's not how it looks. Now hold on to Sunshine's mane, so you don't fall off." He set off along the trail at a trot, leading Sunshine by her reins.

As the pony started forward, Andi felt herself slipping. Hurriedly, she twisted her fingers into Sunshine's mane again. It would be totally humiliating to fall off now. "You don't need to lead me along!" she hissed. "I'm not a complete novice, you know."

Neil ignored her.

"Give me back my reins!" Andi said angrily.

He didn't even glance back, and Andi had no choice but to trot along behind him, feeling angry and shaken and totally fed up. She was beginning to wish her dad hadn't bought her riding lessons after all.

Mrs. Talbot was waiting by the car when Andi and the other riders came clattering into the yard. Buddy began to bark, his tail wagging wildly, but Mrs. Talbot held him firmly by his leash so that he couldn't run over.

Andi was relieved that Neil O'Connor had ridden away once she was back with the group — she would have hated for her mom to see her being led along like a baby. She was still fuming about the way he'd treated her.

"Normally our riders untack their own ponies, but I'll take Sunshine for you," Shona said. "I'd guess you've had enough for today."

"Thanks." Andi handed over the reins, glad that she wouldn't have to take off Sunshine's saddle and bridle herself. She patted the pony. "Thanks, girl." She didn't blame Sunshine for what had happened.

Mrs. O'Connor came out of her office with a man and a woman. "There!" the man said, pointing at Sunshine. "That one's perfect!"

"I'm sorry," Mrs. O'Connor said. "Again, none of my ponies are for sale."

"But our son has his heart set on a buckskin just like that mare," the woman said indignantly.

The man took out his checkbook. "How much? Come on, that pony's just what we want."

"I'm sorry, but I can't help you," Mrs. O'Connor said.

"Come along, Alicia," the man snapped. "And thanks for nothing!" he said gruffly to Mrs. O'Connor. At that, he marched to his SUV, climbed in, and slammed the door. With a final furious glance at Sunshine, his wife followed him.

"Trouble?" Shona asked as the car roared away.

"Just some people who want to buy a buckskin for their son. I've given them the addresses of a couple of farms, but I don't think anyone has a buckskin for sale right now." Mrs. O'Connor shrugged. "Even if I had a pony for sale, I don't think I'd sell it to them after the way they acted!"

Andi hugged Sunshine before she said good-bye. She was glad the pretty mare wasn't going to be sold to such a rude couple.

"How did it go?" asked Mrs. Talbot when Andi ran across to her.

"Not great." Andi crouched down to pet Buddy, and he squirmed onto her lap, overjoyed to see her again.

"Oh? What happened?"

Andi gently pushed Buddy off her lap and stood up. "I don't know. I guess I just don't like riding as much as I thought." There was no way she was going to tell her mom about that horrible Neil O'Connor, who thought he was so great just because he knew everything about ducks and horses! She felt herself blushing just thinking about what had happened.

Mrs. Talbot looked at her quizzically, but to Andi's relief she didn't say any more.

That evening, Andi's dad called. "Tell him I'm out," Andi whispered.

Her mom covered the mouthpiece of the receiver. "No, Andi. He wants to know how your lesson went."

Andi made a face.

"Those lessons cost him a lot of money," Mrs. Talbot whispered. "Tell him you had a great time."

Andi could hardly believe her ears. Her mom had been dead set against the idea of her taking riding lessons, and now she wanted Andi to pretend that her first lesson had gone like something out of a Lassie movie — but with horses. She took the phone. "Hi, Dad."

"Hey, honey. How did it go?"

"Well, the instructor is nice, and the ponies are beautiful — oh, by the way, Mom says thanks for the seeds!"

"I'm glad she likes them. And I'm glad you like your instructor. Listen, I have some great news! I'm going to be in Orchard Park next week for a meeting, so I'll be able to see you on the weekend. In fact, I thought I'd come watch you ride."

Andi bit her lip. She'd have no choice but to go to the stables now — but it would be great to see her dad again.

"I thought you might like to bring a friend along to ride with you," he went on. "We can make a whole day of it — there must be some great places for lunch out in the mountains."

"Oh, yeah! Thanks, Dad. I'll bring my friend Natalie. I told you about her before, remember?" Andi said good-bye to her dad and hung up, just hoping that Neil O'Connor wouldn't be around while she was having her next lesson.

"Want to come riding with me on Saturday morning, Nat?" Andi asked the next day after school. She and Natalie were waiting for Tristan in the schoolyard. He was in a different class than they were, and he often came out a few minutes late.

"Riding's not really my thing." Natalie unzipped her backpack and took out her new peach-flavored lip gloss. "You want to try some of this? It's heavenly!"

"No, thanks."

Andi watched Natalie gloss her lips. "Please come, Nat," she begged. "It'll be great!"

Natalie raised her eyebrows. "Well, if it's really that important to you . . ."

"What's important?" Tristan asked, running up.

Andi linked arms with Natalie. "We're going riding on Saturday."

Tristan frowned. "It's true, then. It really *is* spreading," he said in a voice of doom.

"What is?" Andi and Natalie demanded at the same time.

"Riding disease," Tristan said in a whisper, glancing all around to check that nobody was listening. "The government's trying to keep it quiet, but the news is starting to leak out. First, one person catches it, then another. Before you know it, just about everyone is heading for the stables dressed in ridiculous clothes."

Andi gave him a playful jab in the ribs. "Oh, that reminds me, my dad said I could have some chaps as an early Christmas present!"

"Whoa!" Natalie flipped her ponytail over her shoulder. "I've always wanted a pair of chaps! Suede is totally in this season. Let's go shopping after school tomorrow."

"Shame I can't come and watch you rodeo riding on Saturday," Tristan said. "But I'm helping out at Paws for

Thought." Paws for Thought was the pet store owned by Christine Wilson, Tristan's mom's cousin. Christine often helped the Pet Finders by displaying their posters of lost pets or by giving them information about the type of animal they were searching for.

"Don't worry, Tris," Andi teased. "You should stay away from Hollow Creek anyway — you don't want to catch riding disease!"

Natalie pursed her lips and pretended to look thoughtful. "I don't know, Andi. He could look kind of cute in chaps and a ten-gallon hat!"

After school the next day, Andi and Natalie headed for the sporting goods store. "I looked up riding gear on the Internet last night," Natalie said. "You should have seen some of those chaps. Seriously cool!"

"Are you buying some, too?" Andi asked.

"You bet!"

"But what if you don't like riding? You might decide not to go again."

"I don't want to wear the wrong thing. Chaps will be perfect."

Andi laughed. Natalie had more clothes than a department store! "So, what color do you want?" she said.

"I don't care. Just as long as they're gorgeous."

Andi grinned. She was feeling more upbeat about riding lessons again. They'd be in the sand school — the outdoor arena — this Saturday, and there wouldn't be any snakes there. And with any luck, Neil O'Connor would be out on the trails again. In fact, the more Andi thought about it, the more certain she was that Saturday would be great. Seeing her dad would be terrific — and she'd have new chaps to wear, too!

They found a rack loaded with pairs of chaps — backless leather leggings held together with a belt, to help protect your legs from chafing after a long day in the saddle. Andi was astonished to see how many different designs there were. Some were plain leather or suede, in shades of tan or brown, and others were far fancier, patterned or fringed in a range of colors.

Natalie seized a pair of heavily fringed, scarlet chaps patterned with gold swirls. "These are amazing! What do you think, Andi?"

Before Andi had a chance to reply, Natalie spotted a pair of purple chaps decorated with pink zigzags. "Oh, these are even better!"

Andi stared at her in astonishment. "You're not serious."

"I am. They're awesome!" Natalie pulled them on. "Perfect!"

Shaking her head — and hoping she never ended up sharing Nat's fashion sense — Andi selected a pair of tan chaps patterned in a slightly darker brown. She buckled them on and looked at her reflection with satisfaction.

Natalie wrinkled her nose. "You're not going to buy *them*, are you?"

"What's wrong with them?"

"They're so plain and . . . Oh, look at this!" Natalie darted across the shop and snatched up a suede jacket with fringed sleeves. "I have to have this!" She pulled it on and twirled in front of the mirror, setting the fringes swinging.

"Are you sure?" Andi asked doubtfully. "It looks a bit Annie Oakley-ish. You don't think it's a little over the top?"

"It'll be perfect for riding lessons." Natalie took off the chaps. "And I'll have these, too! Let's go and pay."

Draping the tan chaps over her arm, Andi followed her to the checkout, hoping Natalie's urban cowgirl look wouldn't raise too many eyebrows at Hollow Creek. At this rate, Nat was going to scare the ducks even more than Buddy had!

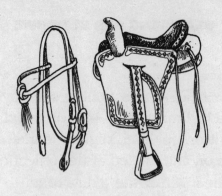

Chapter Four

Andi woke early on Saturday morning. She was going to see her dad! She dragged on her clothes, saving the chaps to put on at the riding center, and ran downstairs with Buddy racing behind her.

"Mom, can I have my breakfast on the porch, so I can watch for Dad?"

"Sure, honey. He said he'd be here about now. Don't forget, he'll be in a rental car."

"Okay!" Andi fed Buddy, grabbed her breakfast muffin, and darted outside. She sat on the top step to eat.

The street was pretty quiet — it was too early for most of the neighbors to be out yet. Two cars passed, but both drivers were women. Then, a blue car turned onto Andi's road. As it approached, Andi spotted her dad in the driver's seat. "Dad!" she yelled, racing down the steps and waving furiously.

David Talbot parked outside Andi's house and jumped out of the car. "Andi! How are you?"

Andi gave him a big hug. "Great, now! Come and see Mom. And Buddy!"

Buddy hurtled out of the living room to greet them, his tail wagging so fast it was just a blur.

Mr. Talbot crouched down to pet him. "How are you, Bud? And how do you like living in Orchard Park?"

"He loves it here," Andi told him.

Buddy barked as though agreeing with her, then began to race in circles around them.

Andi's dad laughed, his dark eyes crinkling. "Calm down, Buddy! You'll make me dizzy."

Judy Talbot came downstairs carrying the vacuum cleaner. "Hey, David. You want some coffee?"

"That would be great."

"Why don't you show your dad your bedroom, Andi, while I make the coffee?"

Andi led the way up the two flights of stairs to her attic bedroom. It was a quirky shape, with sloping ceilings and a dormer window.

"This is great!" her dad said enthusiastically. "I bet you can see the mountaintops from your bed!"

"Only if it's not cloudy. And Orchard Park gets more than its fair share of cloudy days, believe me!"

Mr. Talbot laughed as he followed Andi downstairs again.

"Hey, Dad!" Andi twisted around to look up at him. "You haven't asked about Pet Finders yet! We're not working on a case right now, but we're getting a pretty good reputation around Orchard Park for finding missing pets."

Her dad raised his eyebrows. "Yeah, from your e-mails I guessed there wasn't a cat or a rabbit that could leave home without being pounced on by one of you guys!"

Andi felt a prickle of irritation that her dad didn't seem to be taking their pet finding as seriously as they did, but before she could say anything, her mom appeared with a tray of hot drinks.

"Come and sit in the living room," she invited.

Andi sat on the sofa next to her dad and sipped her hot chocolate. Her mom and dad chatted about work and about the problems of moving to a new town. Andi enjoyed hearing them talk. She knew lots of people whose divorced parents started arguing the minute they saw each other.

"You should get going," Mrs. Talbot said at last. "It takes thirty minutes to get out to Hollow Creek, and you have to pick up Natalie on the way."

Buddy trotted into the hall behind them. "Sorry, Bud,"

Andi said. "You've got to stay with Mom today." She gave him a hug. "Make sure you're a good boy."

"As if he'd be anything else," Mr. Talbot said, appearing in the living room doorway.

Andi darted outside, then stopped to watch her dad come down the steps. She was determined to make today really great.

Natalie ran out of her house as soon as the blue car pulled up outside. She was dressed in her new riding gear, and Andi was startled to see just how bright her chaps were in daylight.

Beaming, Natalie slid into the backseat of the car beside Andi. "Hi, Andi. Is this your dad? Hi, Mr. Talbot. Thanks for inviting me along today."

"Hello, Natalie." Mr. Talbot flashed her a smile in the rearview mirror. "Are you all set?"

"Yep! What do you think of my outfit, Andi?"

Andi shrugged. Her plan to make everything perfect for her dad seemed to be crumbling already: Natalie looked like a contestant for Cowgirl of the Year! "Those chaps are so bright," she said in a low voice. "And all that fringe!"

"What's wrong with them?" Natalie asked in an icy whisper.

"You look like Miss Rodeo!"

Natalie glowered at her. "I do not!" They were still whispering so Andi's dad wouldn't hear.

"Couldn't you just have worn your ordinary jacket?" Andi blurted out. She knew she was making things worse, but she really wanted her dad to like Natalie, not think she was some kind of fashion victim.

"I do know how to dress, Andi. And I happen to think that this outfit is perfect!" Natalie turned away pointedly and stared out of the window.

Andi quickly wished she could take back what she'd said. She placed a hand on Natalie's arm, wanting to apologize, but Natalie shook her off. "Leave me alone."

Andi sat back. She'd say sorry later, when they reached the stables.

"You two are quiet," Mr. Talbot said when they'd been driving awhile.

"We're just thinking about our riding lesson," Natalie said. "Right, Andi?"

"Right." Andi forced a smile. "I can't wait."

"Great! I knew riding lessons would be the perfect gift."

To Andi's dismay, Neil O'Connor was in the yard when they arrived. As if she needed things to get any worse! He watched them climb out of the car. "So you decided to come back? Well, don't worry," he called. "You'll be perfectly safe this time because you're riding in the arena." He swung a headcollar, a simple bitless bridle that could be used to lead horses around, over his shoulder and disappeared into a stable.

Andi felt her cheeks turn bright red.

"What does he mean?" asked Mr. Talbot.

"My pony was spooked by a snake last week." Andi could feel her face growing hotter by the second. "It was no big deal. I wonder which pony Natalie will get to ride?" she said, quickly changing the subject.

Natalie had gone on ahead and was leaning on the rail of the arena. Her back was very stiff and straight, so Andi knew she was still annoyed. She hurried over to her. "Nat, I'm really sorry I said that stuff."

Natalie looked at her. "I guess I might have overdone it a little. Maybe I should have steered clear of fringe." She smiled.

Andi smiled back. "Are we friends again?"

"Sure." Natalie linked arms with her.

Mr. Talbot came over. "It looks like everyone's waiting for you two."

"Right," Andi said, climbing through the rails into the sandy-floored arena. Her dad and Natalie followed. Tim, Helen, and Darryl were there already, sitting on their ponies. Helen was chattering away to nobody in particular about how she wanted to be a famous show jumper when she grew up.

Mrs. O'Connor was holding Sunshine and a brown pony with a black mane and tail that Andi hadn't seen before. She smiled. "Hi, Andi. This must be your dad and Natalie." She and Mr. Talbot shook hands. "I'm in charge of today's lesson. Shona took a party out trail riding."

Natalie put on her riding hat. "Which pony am I riding?"

"Donna, the bay."

Natalie's face lit up. "I love her coat. She's so shiny, I might need shades!"

"Is Sara coming this week?" Andi asked.

"No, she doesn't actually live in Orchard Park. She was just spending last weekend with her aunt. It was her aunt who arranged the lessons for her."

Andi was happy that Natalie was riding Donna, because it meant that she would get Sunshine again. She had really enjoyed riding her last week, in spite of the snake incident.

"Enjoy your lesson," Mr. Talbot said. "I'll watch from the gate."

"Okay." Andi and Natalie mounted their ponies, then waited while Mrs. O'Connor walked out to the center of the arena to start the lesson.

"Welcome, everyone," she said, smiling warmly. She told them to walk around in a circle, using their legs and seat instead of their hands to guide their ponies. "Sit up straight, Tim," Mrs. O'Connor called. "Don't hunch over the pony's neck like that. And hold the reins loosely with one hand. This is Western riding where we steer with our legs, not English where we use the reins more. Think of all those cowboy movies!"

Andi soon found that she was enjoying the lesson and was glad that she'd come.

Suddenly, she realized that Neil was sitting on the fence watching them. She sat up straighter in her saddle, determined to show him that she knew how to ride.

"Change to a trot now," Mrs. O'Connor said. "You should post in time with your pony's stride. That means rise up out of the saddle, one, two, one, two. Up, down, up, down."

Andi gave Sunshine a kick and they broke into a trot. As she was passing Neil, she somehow missed Sunshine's stride and flopped down in the saddle like a fish just as Sunshine's back was rising. It was a silly mistake.

She'd trotted just fine before. Why did she have to mess it up this time, with her dad and Neil watching? Quickly, she corrected herself.

"You're doing well!" Neil called.

Andi glanced over her shoulder in surprise but found that he was talking to Natalie. Andi had to admit that Nat *was* riding well, rising and falling exactly in time with Donna's stride.

Natalie beamed back at Neil.

Great, Andi thought. *It looks as though my best friend's got a crush on my worst enemy!*

"Cantering, now," called Mrs. O'Connor. "It's a little bit quicker than trotting, so you'll need to shorten your reins a little to keep control of your pony."

Andi urged Sunshine into a canter. Usually, she managed to lose a stirrup when she was cantering, but today she succeeded in keeping both feet in place.

"Great job, everyone," Mrs. O'Connor said when they'd all completed a circuit. "That's it for today. Can you all untack your ponies, please? The saddles and bridles go in the tack room at the far end of the stable block." She pointed it out.

Andi slid down from Sunshine's back and patted her. "Good girl, Sunshine." It didn't take long to take off her saddle and bridle, then she made her way over to where

her dad was waiting. He smiled broadly at her. "Good job, Andi. You looked great out there."

Before Andi could reply, Natalie came tearing across the yard with her riding helmet under her arm. "Neil says he'll show us around the farm, Andi!"

Andi's heart sank. She didn't want to hang out with the Neil-and-Natalie mutual fan club. "There won't be time. We have to go to lunch."

"Well, I'm in no hurry," Mr. Talbot said. "I'd love to have a look around."

Neil came over. "Are you ready?"

Natalie ran her hands through her long blond hair and tucked a wayward strand behind her ear. "You bet! I've always been interested in farms."

Andi gaped at her in disbelief. A farmyard was the last place Natalie would choose to hang out! She was always so concerned about her designer clothes that she wouldn't want to be within a million miles of a muddy field! But even though she'd just been riding, she still looked cool and immaculate. Andi sighed. She was boiling hot, and she knew her face must be red. There was a wet patch on her sweater, too, where Sunshine had dribbled on her.

"I'll show you the goats first." Neil led them to the

barn. Mr. Talbot stopped to talk to Shona, who had just ridden into the yard. Andi trailed along behind Natalie and Neil, feeling like a spare part.

"Oh, they're adorable!" Natalie exclaimed as they went into the barn.

The cute, fluffy goat that Andi had petted before was lying by the fence again. It stood up when it saw her and she leaned over the rail to pet it. To her amazement, Natalie started stroking the goats as well and didn't even flinch when one of them started nibbling the fringe on her jacket.

"Come and look at the duck pond," Neil said after a few minutes. "The ducks are mine. It's my project for the 4-H Club."

"No way! I always wanted to join the 4-H Club," Natalie gushed, following Neil out.

Andi stared at her. "No, you haven't!"

"Yes, I have!" She grinned. "You don't know everything about me, Andi." Turning to Neil again, she said, "I'm really committed to animals. That's why I helped set up the Pet Finders Club with Andi and our friend Tristan. Maybe you've heard of it? We've dealt with some pretty high profile cases of lost pets."

Neil looked at Andi as though he expected her to join

in the conversation, but she pretended she hadn't noticed. There was no way she was going to make friends with Mr. High-and-Mighty Neil O'Connor!

"It sounds like a great idea!" Neil said enthusiastically, turning to Natalie again. "Tell me about some of your cases."

"Oh, we've found tons of missing animals — cats, dogs, guinea pigs. Once we even tracked down some stolen lizards. We haven't had a case yet that we couldn't solve."

"Give me your phone number, and if anyone's lost a pet I can tell them who to call," Neil said.

"Here you go." Natalie pulled out a handful of flyers advertising the Pet Finders Club. Normally, the flyers included Andi's cell phone number, but they had Natalie's now, since Andi had broken hers during an early morning run.

"These are cool! I'll put some in my mom's office and some around the stables for students to take," Neil suggested. He and Natalie walked away.

Andi stayed where she was. She watched the ducks swimming around on the pond for a while, then went to find her dad. Hopefully, he'd say it was time to go to lunch. Andi wanted to get away from Neil as soon as she possibly could!

* * *

The diner Mr. Talbot took Andi and Natalie to was cute, with red-and-white gingham curtains and tablecloths. They sat at the counter on seats made from real saddles. They all ordered burgers and fries and banana shakes. While they ate, Mr. Talbot chatted about his upcoming trip overseas to deal with some problems on an oil rig.

After lunch, they dropped off Natalie at her house, then drove to Andi's. "I can't come in," he said as he drew up outside. "I've got to get to the airport for my flight to Asia."

Andi hugged him. "Thanks for coming, Dad. It's been great to see you."

"I'll send you a postcard."

"Okay. And I'll get Mom to take some digital pictures of me riding, so I can e-mail them to you."

"Great! I'll give you a call as soon as I get home."

"I love you!" Andi suddenly felt very lonely as she watched him drive away. It was really hard, only seeing him a few times a year. She loved living with her mom — and Buddy — but she missed her dad very much.

Chapter Five

When she got to school Monday morning, Andi looked around for Natalie and Tristan.

Natalie waved to her from behind a group of sixth graders. "Hi, Andi," she called. "Wow! Great weekend! You didn't tell me about Neil. He is *so* cute."

Andi blinked. Natalie obviously had a crush!

"Thanks for taking me riding with you," Natalie went on. "I never would have met him if it weren't for you."

Andi made a face. "Are you kidding?"

"No, he's terrific! You have to let me come with you again next week," Natalie said. "I asked my mom and dad and they said it was okay."

Andi wasn't sure what to say. She could hardly say no — riding with a friend would be fun. But she wasn't keen on the idea of watching Nat and Neil fawn over each other. Especially when Neil probably still thought she was a lousy rider.

Natalie clutched her arm. "I'm relying on you, Andi. I can't get to the stables alone. My dad plays golf every Saturday morning and my mom goes to her bridge club. And I want you as a riding buddy!"

Andi relented. "Okay. I'm sure my mom won't mind."

Natalie smiled. "Thanks, Andi." She linked arms with her. "Now tell me everything you know about Neil. And don't leave out a thing!"

While the Pet Finders were in the schoolyard at lunchtime on Thursday, standing with their backs to the bitter wind, Natalie's cell phone rang. She looked down at the caller ID and her face brightened. "It's Neil!"

He must be serious, thought Andi. Beside her, Tristan rolled his eyes. He was obviously getting tired of hearing about the amazing Neil O'Connor, too.

Natalie answered the phone with a cheery, "Hi there!" but quickly looked serious. "Neil, that's terrible!" She paused, listening. "Of course we'll help, but we won't be able to get there until Saturday. okay. See you then." She snapped her phone shut and slipped it into her bag.

"What happened?" Andi asked.

"One of the ponies has disappeared! Neil wants us to help find her." Natalie slid an arm around Andi's shoulders. "I'm sorry, Andi. It's Sunshine."

Andi was shocked. "Oh, no! We need to get to Hollow Creek right now!"

"Not likely," Tristan pointed out. "The bell will ring for seventh period any minute now, and we won't find a pony before then," he added. "They may be bigger than your average dog or cat, but I bet they can travel farther."

"I can't believe Sunshine might be out on the mountainside, lost and alone," Andi said with a sigh.

"Maybe not on the mountain," Natalie said. "Neil says she could have been stolen."

"Stolen!" Andi stared at Natalie in horror. "That's even worse!"

"Well, we're the right people to tackle the case," Tristan said. "We've got a great track record. Though we should try to steer clear of any thieves." He was clearly remembering the trouble they got into with the thief who had raided Christine's store.

"The police are investigating," Natalie added, "but they haven't found her yet."

"Poor Sunshine," Andi said sadly. "I hope we can get her back!"

* * *

Andi was up extra early Saturday morning, though she'd stayed up late the night before checking the Internet for articles about horse thieves. She rushed downstairs to help with the chores so that she and her mom could leave for the stables as soon as possible.

Mr. Peters dropped off Natalie at Andi's house just before nine o'clock. "Don't come in," Andi said as she opened the door. "We're leaving right now." She clipped on Buddy's leash and called to her mom.

"Hurry up!" Natalie exclaimed impatiently. She was wearing a denim jacket with blue jeans tucked into suede boots. Her hair was held back with a lilac hairband.

Mrs. Talbot came hurrying downstairs. "All set. Let's go."

Andi and Natalie dashed to the car and dove into the backseat; Buddy leaped in after them.

"Isn't Tristan coming with you?" Mrs. Talbot asked as she reversed out of the driveway.

"He's helping out at Paws for Thought today," Natalie replied. "But he gave me a huge list of things to find out about while we're at the stables."

"Did you call Mrs. O'Connor, Andi, to cancel your riding lesson?"

"Yes. I told her we want to help find Sunshine. She said the police haven't come up with anything yet."

"We'll solve this puzzle," Natalie said confidently. "We haven't been beaten yet."

The journey to the stables seemed to take forever.

Neil ran out to meet them when they drove into the yard. He was wearing a battered stable coat, muddy jeans, and sturdy rubber boots. "Thanks for coming!" he said. "I'll tell you what happened while I feed the goats."

"What time should I come get you?" asked Mrs. Talbot as Andi and Natalie scrambled out of the car.

"It's okay, Mom, we can get the bus. Natalie found one that runs from the end of the road right back to Orchard Park. It stops right outside Rocky's store."

"That's convenient," said her mom. "And it will give me the chance to take Buddy for a walk. That way, you won't have to rush home."

Andi beamed at her, appreciating the way she took pet finding as seriously as they did. "Thanks, Mom!"

"Don't leave the farm, though, okay?"

"Okay. See you later, Mom. And you, too, Buddy!" Andi patted Buddy, gave her mom a quick kiss, and darted after Natalie and Neil, who were heading for the barn.

"Sunshine was in the far paddock when she disappeared," Neil began. He stopped at a tiny storeroom full of animal food and pulled out a bag of flaked grain. "The goats need extra food this time of year because there's not enough grass for them," he explained. He led the way into the barn, tossed the bag of feed over the barrier, and climbed in after it. The black-and-white goats milled around him, bleating excitedly. "All right!" He threaded his way between them, tucking the bag under one arm and ripping it open with his free hand. "I'm going as fast as I can!"

"Were there any other ponies in the paddock?" Natalie asked.

"Bonnie, Chipper, Donna, and Scrumpy." Neil tipped food into the first trough. The goats gathered around, nudging one another aside in their determination to eat first. "And my horse, Flash. Oh, and Tilly. But the thief only took Sunshine."

"The thief left Flash and Tilly?" Andi asked with surprise.

"I know. Those two are much more valuable than Sunshine." Neil glanced at her and shook his head as if he couldn't understand it, either. Then he headed for another trough, with a line of goats skittering behind him. "The police thought it was weird, too. They wondered if the thief had been interrupted, but we didn't hear the dogs barking or the ducks quacking."

Natalie looked at him in surprise. "Ducks?"

"Ducks and geese make great watchdogs. They're very suspicious of strangers and can make a real racket if they don't like the look of someone. But not in this case."

"When did you find out Sunshine was missing?" Natalie questioned.

"Thursday morning. We often leave the horses and ponies out overnight if it's not too cold. There's a really solid barn in that paddock. The horses can go right inside, and they all wear blankets at night this time of year, anyway." He filled the last trough and trudged back. "They don't like being cooped up in the stable much, but we've been bringing them in at about four o'clock since Sunshine disappeared."

"Can we have a look at the paddock?" Andi said.

"I'll take you there now."

Andi and Natalie followed him outside and along the narrow pathway that ran between the barn and the stables. Andi felt her cheeks go red as they passed the duck pond, remembering how Buddy had chased the ducks just before she had her first run-in with Neil. *He seems different today*, she thought, *a bit quieter and less sure of himself*. He obviously cared about his animals.

"We have to go across the cow pasture to reach the far paddock," Neil warned. "Are you both okay with cows?"

"I am," Andi told him.

Natalie was walking beside Neil, but she glanced back at Andi and made a horrified face. Andi bit her lip, trying not to giggle.

Neil didn't notice. "I guess *you* like cows, Natalie," he said, "if you've been thinking of joining 4-H."

"What? Oh, yes. I love them," Natalie replied in a rush. "They're so . . . um . . . cute."

"Cute? Well, I guess you could call them that." Neil gave her an odd look, then opened the gate. Natalie stayed close to him as they crossed the field, but the cows took little notice of them; they just went on contentedly munching grass.

They reached the far side of the field and let themselves into the paddock through a five-barred gate. Andi looked around, trying to take in everything. *If only Tristan were here*, she thought. With his amazing memory, they wouldn't miss a single detail.

In the middle of the paddock stood a sturdy stone building with a narrow doorway just wide enough to let a horse through. Two ponies, Tilly and Scrumpy, were cropping the grass on the sheltered side of the barn. Three more ponies and Neil's palomino, Flash, were standing in a huddle a little way off. The paddock had a wooden post-and-rail fence on three sides, with two gates — the one they'd just come through and another opening out onto the mountainside. Andi made a mental note to check that there were no loose rails that might have let Sunshine slip out. The river ran along the fourth side of the paddock.

Natalie hung back to speak to Andi as Neil headed toward the barn. She took out Tristan's list and read the first item. "He wants us to look for tire tracks. Could a thief have brought a truck up here, do you think?"

"The gates are wide enough. And if he cut across the fields instead of driving through the stable yard, it would explain why Neil and his mom didn't hear anything."

"Let's go check the gates, then."

"I wish Tris were here," Andi said as they jogged back to the first gate. "He's really good at spotting things."

"You're right, but don't say that when he's around," Natalie warned with a grin. "You'll only feed his ego."

The ground around the gateway was soft and a bit muddy in places. They found plenty of hoofprints, but no tire tracks. "Maybe some of these hoofprints are Sunshine's," Andi said. "But how can we tell?"

Natalie shrugged. "I don't know, but I'm beginning to see why Neil wears old clothes. My jeans are muddy already, and we've only been here a few minutes. I am *so* going to need a bath when I get home. And a washing machine!"

Andi laughed. "Let's check the other gate." As she raced away, a fine drizzle began to fall.

"Hang on, Andi!" Natalie called.

"What?" Andi spun around and ran back. "Did you find something?"

"No. But there doesn't seem much point in both of us getting wet. Maybe someone should go check out the barn."

Andi raised her eyebrows. "And you're volunteering, I bet."

"Somebody has to do it."

"Go on. I'll meet you in there." Andi pulled up her hood, then sped away.

There were no tire tracks by the gate that led up to the mountain, either. Andi didn't know whether to be disappointed or relieved. If Sunshine had been taken away in a truck, then she could be anywhere by now — maybe even in another state. But if she'd gotten away on foot, she could be lost on the mountain, where she could get herself hurt or stuck. Andi stared up at the pine forests stretching away, suddenly afraid that if Sunshine were somewhere in there, she might never be found.

Chapter Six

Andi blinked her eyes against the rain, wishing that when she opened them again, she would see the pretty buckskin trotting down the mountainside toward her. But there was no sign of any animals at all, aside from a speck in the sky that might have been a circling hawk.

"Don't worry, Sunshine," she whispered, determined not to be downhearted. "We'll find you." But she couldn't help wondering how, when they didn't have a single clue so far.

She checked the gate. The latch was well-oiled and held fast even when Andi threw all her weight against it. She tested the hinges, too, wondering if Sunshine might have pushed her way out — the Pet Finders had once tracked down a cat that had escaped through a screen door with a broken hinge. But the metal fittings weren't damaged in any way, and the gate held firmly to its post.

Sighing, Andi jogged down to the barn, where she found Natalie making notes on the back of a store receipt. "So what was the exact time when you found the pony gone?" she asked Neil, sounding like a detective — or Tristan.

"Just before seven-thirty in the morning."

Natalie scribbled this down. "Oh, hi, Andi. Any luck?"

"No."

Natalie frowned, then returned to questioning Neil. "Did you see anything unusual? Were either of the gates open, maybe?"

"No, nothing. Everything was exactly the same as it always is, except that Sunshine wasn't here. Shona saw something when she was on her way into work Thursday morning, though. She passed a big green horse truck. She said it was speeding, and she had to swerve to avoid it."

"Did she see the license plate?" Andi asked eagerly.

"No. She didn't know Sunshine was missing then, so it didn't seem important. But she noticed that it had a huge dent on the left side of the fender, with a big scrape of red paint across it."

Natalie wrote down the details. "I bet Sunshine was inside that truck, and that the thief was trying to make a quick getaway!"

"It definitely sounds suspicious," Andi agreed. "And a truck like that should be pretty easy to recognize — as long as they don't get the dent fixed." At least it would give them something to work on, she thought. Maybe they could check out farms around Orchard Park to see if anyone had a dented truck.

"The police thought it might have been the thief, too," Neil said. "They said they'd keep an eye out for it."

"So, what do we do now?" Natalie asked. "Start searching for the truck?"

"Not yet," Andi replied. "We don't know for sure that Sunshine was inside. Let's finish here first. We should look at the fence. Maybe there's a break in it somewhere and the rail kind of bounced back in place after Sunshine had escaped."

Neil's eyebrows shot up, almost disappearing into his hair. "I'm sure we'd have noticed if there was something wrong with the fence."

"It's worth checking, though," Andi insisted.

Natalie looked out through the open doorway. "It's raining harder now." She wrinkled her nose. "I don't want to smudge my notes. Tris would never forgive me."

"Put them in your pocket," Andi said. She moved close to Natalie and lowered her voice. "You don't want Neil thinking you're scared of a little rain, do you?" she teased.

Natalie gave an indignant sniff, then stuffed the receipt in her pocket. "I guess we *should* check out the fence." Turning up her collar, she followed Andi outside.

They walked slowly around the edge of the paddock, checking the rails for signs of damage. Here and there, where the wood was rough and splintery, they found a few strands of coarse pony hair in various colors.

"This looks like Sunshine's hair," Natalie said excitedly, gathering a few coppery strands.

"That doesn't mean anything," Neil warned. "The ponies stand against the fence all the time. Their hair just gets snagged."

"I'll keep it, anyway. We might need to match it against another clump of hair later." Natalie placed the hair carefully in her pocket. "We had to do that once before, for a puppy we found."

"What about the river?" Andi said. "Could Sunshine have waded across?"

"It's way too deep," Neil said.

All the same, they went to have a closer look. But as Neil had said, it was very deep and fast-flowing, too.

"You don't think she could have fallen in?" Andi asked with a shiver. No animal would have stood a chance in that swift current.

"No way! Sunshine's really surefooted," Neil said. "In

any case, the horses don't need to go to the river, even if they're thirsty. There's a water trough just outside the barn door."

Andi walked along the riverbank while Natalie stood near the fence with Neil and drew a plan of the paddock on the back of Tristan's list. She held the paper close to her chest to shield it from the rain. To Andi's relief, there were no hoofprints anywhere near the water. But if it was so hard for the ponies to get out of the paddock on their own, it was looking more and more likely that Sunshine had been stolen. And if the green horse truck hadn't come from a local farm, she could be anywhere!

"Well, that's that," Natalie said when Andi returned. "We've got only one clue. I really hope it turns out to be a good one, because otherwise . . . " She shrugged.

Neil gulped. "You don't think we're going to find her, do you?" He turned away to fiddle with a splinter on the fence. "I'm so worried about her."

"We'll do our best," Andi said gently, squeezing his arm. Neil might be sharp with people, but he was clearly concerned about his animals.

He nodded and rubbed his eyes with his sleeve, then glanced at his watch. "I promised Mom that I'd take some of the ponies back to the yard for her. Are you finished?"

"Yep." Natalie put away her pen and shook raindrops from her hair.

"I'll go get the ponies, then." Neil vanished into the barn, reappearing a moment later with three rope halters. He delved into his pocket and brought out a chunk of carrot. Holding it on the flat of his hand, he walked toward Tilly and Scrumpy. They watched him approach, then Scrumpy trotted over, her ears pricked eagerly.

Neil rubbed her nose. "I can always rely on you, Scrumpy." He glanced over his shoulder at Andi and Natalie. "She's crazy about carrots."

Andi thought about Sunshine. She hoped whoever had taken her was feeding her well.

Scrumpy took the carrot and, while she was chewing, Neil slipped the halter over her head. "Natalie, can you hang on to Scrumpy? I'll catch the others."

It took Neil only a few moments to slip the remaining two halters onto Tilly and Chipper. "Here, Andi." Neil handed her Tilly's halter rope, and they led the three ponies across the paddock to the gate.

As they crossed the cow pasture, Andi noticed a smear of mud on Tilly's neck. She brushed it away. Underneath the mud, there was a triangle of white hair with an H inside that stood out against the pony's chestnut coat.

She glanced at Scrumpy and Chipper; they weren't quite as muddy, and neither of them seemed to have a brand. "How come Tilly's branded but these other two aren't?"

"Most of our horses are freeze-branded," Neil replied. "It identifies the horses as ours. But we haven't had Scrumpy or Chipper long. We're waiting for someone to come and do it."

"What about Sunshine? Is she branded?"

"Yes."

Andi's heart began to beat faster. "But that doesn't make sense. Why didn't the thief take an unbranded horse that couldn't be traced?"

"I know. It's weird," Neil agreed. "And most thieves would take all the horses in one field at the same time. If you're only going to take one, why take one that's branded?"

Natalie peered closer at Tilly's brand. "How does it work?"

"Every horse owner has an iron cut in their own style of brand," Neil explained. "It's frozen onto the horse's skin and it makes the hair grow back differently. It's

usually a different color, and the texture of the hair changes, too."

Natalie shuddered. "It sounds horrible!"

"No, it doesn't really hurt. People say it's equivalent to girls having their ears pierced."

"So when someone tries to sell the horse, buyers can check that it hasn't been stolen?" Natalie asked. She touched Tilly's brand gingerly as though she were afraid of hurting her.

Neil nodded. "There's a national register of brands. It makes selling a stolen horse that's branded pretty tricky."

"This could be a really important clue." Natalie gripped Andi's arm. "We must be looking for an inexperienced thief who doesn't know much about horses."

"Or someone who only steals one horse at a time," Andi said. "Like someone who works alone or only has a small truck."

Natalie looked doubtful.

"Well, it's possible!" Andi said defensively.

"Maybe we could look through some horse journals," Natalie suggested. "We could read up on past thefts to see if there are any similarities."

"I think Mom has a whole stack in the office," Neil offered.

As soon as the ponies were handed over to their riders, Andi, Natalie, and Neil hurried to Mrs. O'Connor's office. It was a small room, the walls crammed with photos of horses and riders.

Andi and Natalie sat on a lumpy sofa to one side of the desk while Neil opened the bottom drawer of the filing cabinet. "You Pet Finders really seem to know what you're doing," he said, taking out a pile of magazines. He put them on the sofa between Andi and Natalie, then perched on the desk. They began to leaf through the magazines, starting with the most recent, but nearly all the reports of thefts referred to all the horses and ponies in one paddock being taken at the same time.

"How could they take them all?" Natalie asked. "Wouldn't the thieves need a whole fleet of horse trucks?"

"No. Not if they didn't mind cramming them in," Neil said. "Some of those big trucks would hold about twelve horses if they were squashed together. And you wouldn't find more than that in an average paddock."

They went on reading, but the only individual horses that had been stolen were famous show jumpers.

"Maybe some horses are stolen to order?" Natalie suggested, looking up from her magazine. "You know, like paintings."

Andi and Neil stared at her blankly.

"If a crooked art collector wants a particular painting, they can pay someone to steal it," Natalie went on. "Then they hang it in their private collection and nobody knows where it's gone. Maybe it's the same with horses. People could steal top-class horses and breed from them, even if they had to keep the stolen horse secret."

"Sunshine's a lovely pony, but she's not famous or really well-bred," Andi pointed out.

"I guess whoever took her might have wanted a regular riding pony," Neil said. "But then, why didn't they take an unbranded pony?"

Natalie shrugged. "Maybe Sunshine was the easiest to catch."

They went on scouring the magazines for another half hour. "This is hopeless!" Andi said at last. She straightened up, rubbing her back. "I don't suppose you have a photo of Sunshine, do you, Neil?"

"Sure." He took one down from the wall next to the window and handed it to her. The pretty buckskin mare was standing in the yard, looking straight at the camera with her ears pricked.

"Hang on!" Andi exclaimed. "What about that couple who wanted a buckskin pony for their son?"

Neil and Natalie looked at her blankly.

"Didn't your mom mention them, Neil? They were here the day of my first lesson." Andi felt herself blushing as she remembered the way Neil had rescued her that day when Sunshine bolted. "I just remembered. They were pretty upset when your mom said Sunshine wasn't for sale." She stood up. "Let's go talk to her about them."

They found Mrs. O'Connor in the tack room, cleaning a saddle. "Can you tell us anything about that rude couple who wanted to buy Sunshine?" Andi asked.

"We think they might have stolen her," Natalie added.

Mrs. O'Connor frowned. "Oh, I don't know. You honestly think they'd steal her?" She paused. "They *were* very insistent. I should mention them to the police."

"Did you get their names?" Neil said. "Or where they live?"

His mother shook her head. "No. I don't really know anything about them. Except that they've got a son who wants a buckskin pony. And their car's some kind of big SUV."

"It was blue," Andi said. She thought hard, trying to recall more details, but she'd been so upset about her disastrous riding lesson that day, she hadn't paid much attention. "I don't know what make their car was. They were both tall, but I can't even think what color hair they had or what they were wearing. Oh, this is ridiculous — there must be thousands of tall people with blue SUVs in the area!"

"Sorry I can't be of more help," Mrs. O'Connor said. She put down her cleaning cloth. "But I *am* going to go call the police."

Andi, Natalie, and Neil trailed back to the office and delved into the horse magazines again.

"We should go," Natalie said, looking at her watch. "Otherwise we'll miss the bus."

"Okay." Andi stood up. As she slipped on her coat, a headline in one of the magazines that was open on the table caught her eye.

RIDERS LEFT HORSELESS AFTER THEFT FROM LIVERY STABLES, it read. Andi picked up the magazine. There was a photo of some kids standing in an empty field, looking miserable. Andi scanned the article. All the ponies had been stolen in a night raid on the stables. She glanced at the photo again and this time she gasped in astonishment.

"Look at this!" She waved the magazine under Neil's nose. "Don't you recognize someone in this photo? It's Sara!"

Chapter Seven

"I met Sara when I came for my first lesson here," Andi explained to Nat. "Maybe she can give us a few tips about finding stolen ponies! She might have gotten her pony back in the end. Do you have her address, Neil?"

"Well, she was staying with her aunt when she came here." Neil opened the filing cabinet and took out a large book. He flipped through the pages until he found what he was looking for. "Here it is. Her aunt's name is Hannah Walker. She lives at Halfpenny Farm on Boundary Road in Orchard Park."

"I know where that is!" Andi said. "Tris and I went down that way with his dad a couple of weeks ago to photograph some real estate. We can go over on our bikes when we get back to town, Nat."

"Good idea," Natalie agreed. "Isn't it weird how it's

harder to find a big animal like a horse than a tiny guinea pig?"

"You *are* going to stick with it, aren't you?" Neil asked anxiously.

"Of course we are. We'll do everything we can."

Andi heard a note of uncertainty in Natalie's voice and realized that she was starting to feel discouraged. "We've never failed with a case yet," Andi said, trying to reassure her. "And we're not going to start now."

"Thanks," Neil said. "I'm really grateful."

Natalie glanced at her watch and gave a squeal. "Come on!" She yanked Andi to her feet. "Bye, Neil! I'll call you as soon as we get any news."

"Let us know if you hear anything, too!" Andi called over her shoulder as Natalie rushed her out the door.

As soon as they got back to Orchard Park, Andi and Natalie got their bikes and rode to Halfpenny Farm. It was on the very edge of town, not too far from Andi's house. The farmhouse, a colonial-style building with green shutters and a wide veranda, was set back from the road at the end of a long driveway that ran between fields of apple trees, with fallen leaves littering the ground beneath them.

"I remember coming here when I lost Buddy," Andi

said. "I thought he might have run into the trees, and I called for ages, but he wasn't here."

She and Natalie leaned their bikes against the veranda railing. "I hope someone's home after that ride," Natalie said, short of breath.

Andi laughed. "Exercise is good for you, Nat."

"It might be good for *you*, but sitting around suits *me* just fine, thanks."

As they climbed onto the veranda, the front door opened and a tall gray-haired woman stepped out carrying a suitcase. She stopped dead when she saw Andi and Natalie. "Can I help you?"

"We were hoping you could give us Sara's phone number," Andi said. "You're Mrs. Walker, aren't you?"

The woman dropped her suitcase. "You know Sara?" she gasped.

"Not very well," Andi admitted, puzzled by the woman's reaction. "We went trail riding together at Hollow Creek Riding Center."

Mrs. Walker sighed and picked up her case again.

"Is something wrong?" Natalie asked.

Mrs. Walker looked very grave. "I'm sorry to tell you this, but Sara ran away three days ago. Someone saw her waiting at a Greyhound bus stop near her home."

Andi stared in dismay.

"I'm off to stay with my sister's family now," Mrs. Walker continued. "I would have gone sooner, but I had to wait until my husband got back from a trip. What did you want to speak to Sara about?"

"We're trying to find a stolen pony," Natalie explained. "We knew Sara's pony was stolen last year and we thought she might be able to give us some tips on finding this one."

"It's not important now, though," Andi added quickly. "Don't let us hold you up."

"No. I'd better get going. I want to get there before dark." Mrs. Walker headed to a pickup truck that was parked to one side of the farmhouse. She put her suitcase on the passenger seat, then turned to Andi and Natalie again. "I think Sara went to lots of horse sales to try to get her pony back. Maybe you could try that." She climbed into the truck and drove away.

"Whoa!" Natalie said, wide-eyed. "Missing pets are one thing, but missing people . . . that's a whole other ball game! Why do you think she ran away?"

"I don't know, but I hope she's okay." She bit her lip. Usually, that was what she'd say about missing animals — it was even scarier to be saying it about a person.

* * *

On Sunday morning, Natalie called Andi right after breakfast. "Guess what? There's a horse sale on the other side of town today. My mom says she'll give us a ride."

"Okay," said Andi. "I've been thinking about Sara, too, wondering if we can do anything to help find her, but I haven't come up with any ideas."

"Me, neither. But the police and her family must be searching for her all over. If they can't find her, I don't see how we can be much use. We might as well keep looking for Sunshine. This sale might be just the place."

"Yeah, you're right." What Natalie said made a lot of sense: They didn't have the slightest idea where Sara might have gone, so how could they hope to help? "We'll stick to finding Sunshine and hope Sara turns up soon."

Mrs. Talbot came into the hall. "Is there news about Sunshine?"

Andi quickly told her mom about the sale. "Is it okay to go?"

"Of course. Just make sure you're home in time to take Buddy for a walk."

Buddy seemed to sense Andi's excitement as she hurried to get ready. He raced around her, giving little high-pitched barks. "I'm sorry, Bud. I can't take you with me."

Through the window, Andi saw Natalie's mom pull up

outside. She gave Buddy a quick hug, then ran to put on her coat. "Bye, Mom! See you later." She darted out to the car, leaving Buddy watching her mournfully from the living-room window.

The horse sale was bustling with people. Andi looked at the excited faces around her and thought how strange it was that she and Natalie were here for a sad reason, to find a pony that might have been stolen.

"Let's start over there," Natalie suggested, grabbing Andi's arm and steering her through the crowd. A bunch of little kids were clustered around the first pen, admiring a tiny Shetland pony. Andi wished they could stop, but they didn't have time. Natalie's mom was reading a magazine in the car and Andi didn't want to make her wait for ages.

They squeezed through the crush of people to the next pen. A pair of enormous chestnut horses stood there, restlessly pawing the ground. "Keep going," Natalie urged. "It looks like there's a clearing up ahead."

They passed more horses and ponies but, to Andi's disappointment, none of them looked like Sunshine.

Soon they reached a wide fenced-off auction arena. There were several ponies in the collecting ring on the far side, waiting to be sold. As Andi watched, they shifted and she saw a flash of copper-colored hair. "Over there!" she said excitedly. "I'm sure one of those ponies is a buckskin." She grabbed Natalie's hand and dragged her between two men who were talking loudly about the price of a quarter horse colt.

"What's a quarter horse?" Natalie asked. "It sounds like it just has one leg or something!"

"It's a breed of horse that can run a quarter of a mile really fast," Andi explained.

Natalie gaped at her, clearly impressed.

Andi grinned. "I just read it yesterday in one of Neil's horse magazines."

They wriggled through the crowd around the edge of the auction area, but when they reached the collecting ring, they could see that the buckskin was just over four feet high. "That's not her," Andi said, disappointed. "Sunshine's taller."

"There are a couple more buckskins down here," Natalie said. "Come on."

As they made their way along beside the pens, Andi spotted the couple who'd tried to buy Sunshine from Mrs. O'Connor. "It's them!" she gasped. "The people who wanted Sunshine. Let's follow them!"

"Do you think they've brought her here to sell her?" Natalie asked as they squeezed through the crowd, try-

ing to keep the couple in sight. "Maybe they were lying when they said they wanted to buy her for their son."

The couple stopped by a pen containing a pair of buckskin ponies, but neither of them was Sunshine. Andi and Natalie moved closer, wanting to hear what they said. "How much are they?" the woman asked.

Andi couldn't hear the owner's reply, but the man took out his checkbook immediately. "We'll take the one on the right," he said. "He'll love it!"

"They're not selling," Natalie said with a frustrated sigh. "They really are buying a pony for their son."

Suddenly, Andi heard someone calling her name. Glancing around, she saw Neil and Mrs. O'Connor hurrying toward them. "It looks like you had the same idea we did," said Mrs. O'Connor.

"Have you found her yet?" Natalie asked.

"Not yet," Neil replied. "But there are a lot of buckskins here. Maybe we'll get lucky. Did you speak to Sara?"

"No. Get this—she ran away!" Andi said.

"Ran away?" Neil echoed, shocked.

"That's terrible!" Mrs. O'Connor exclaimed. "What made her do it, I wonder?"

"Maybe she had a fight with her parents or something," Natalie said. "Anyway, we should keep searching for Sunshine so nobody buys her."

While they worked their way along the pens, Andi told Neil and his mom about seeing the couple who'd wanted to buy Sunshine. The four of them stopped at every buckskin and looked it over carefully. Quite a few resembled Sunshine at first, but when they looked closer, they found that they were just too tall or too short or a fraction too stocky or too thin. And none of them had dark streaks in their tails.

"She's not here," Andi said at last. "We've looked in every single pen."

"It was a long shot," Mrs. O'Connor admitted. "Even if the thieves do plan to sell Sunshine, they'll probably wait until people have stopped looking for her. She might not appear in a sale for months."

Andi looked at Neil's tense, unhappy face and a wave of sympathy washed over her. She'd been heartbroken when she'd lost Buddy, so she knew exactly how he felt.

"Thanks for trying," Mrs. O'Connor said. "Neil told me about your Pet Finders Club and I really appreciate the effort you're making." She sighed. "I'm not sure we're going to get her back, though. It's beginning to look like she's vanished into thin air."

Andi's school was closed on Monday for parent-teacher conferences, so she and Natalie took the bus to Hollow

Creek. Buddy went with them, firmly clipped to his leash. They planned to go up the mountain this time, on the chance that Sunshine had somehow gotten out of the paddock on her own. Andi knew Buddy would enjoy the walk.

"It's a shame Tristan couldn't come," Natalie said as they got off the bus outside the stables. He'd promised to help Christine with a big delivery of feed at the pet store.

"We'll call him if we find anything," Andi promised.

Neil was mucking out the stables when they reached the yard. "Hi!" Natalie called.

He whirled around, nearly stabbing himself in the foot with his pitchfork. "Did you find her?"

"Not yet. We're going to look for her on the mountain. What are you doing here, anyway? We thought you'd be at school today."

"Conferences. Is that why you're off, too?"

"Yep."

He glanced at his watch. "If you can hang around for twenty minutes, I'll come with you. I've got a few chores to finish first."

"Maybe we could give you a hand," Andi suggested. "It'll be quicker if we all help."

"Great! I'll get a couple of brooms." Neil disappeared into the stable.

"Thanks, Andi," Natalie said sarcastically. "I've always wanted to clean a stable. *Not!*"

"Sorry. But it would be good if Neil came, too. It's getting cloudy, and I don't like the idea of being out on the mountain when rain is bucketing down."

Natalie took off her coat. "I'm not going to risk getting this dirty. I've only had it a couple of weeks." She draped it over the lower half of the stable door.

Andi gaped at her. "What on earth are you wearing?"

"Overalls."

Andi stared. Natalie was always buying clothes, so it was surprising to see her dressed in anything that was more than a month old. But these overalls looked ancient. Made of faded denim, they were patched and worn, and the buttons didn't match.

"Where did you get them?"

"They're my mom's."

Now Andi was even more astonished. She had never seen Natalie's mom, who was a successful interior designer, wear anything but gorgeous, high-fashion clothing.

Natalie saw the look of disbelief on Andi's face. "Mom

thinks she might have to pitch in with the painting one day if a decorator lets her down." She grinned. "There's not much chance of that, though, if you ask me. She knows hundreds of painters. Do you think I've overdone the whole country look?" Natalie suddenly looked anxious.

"Well, you certainly look different," Andi admitted.

"But is it too much?"

Before Andi had a chance to reply, Neil reappeared carrying two brooms. He handed one to Natalie and the other to Andi. "We need to sweep the last of the straw out of the stable, and then put in some fresh stuff. You can tie Buddy's leash to this hook, Andi. That should keep him out of mischief."

"He's not going to misbehave today," Andi promised, ruffling Buddy's ears. "You're going to be a really good boy, aren't you, Bud?"

"I'll believe that when I see it," Neil muttered darkly.

Andi felt a flash of irritation. *Trust Neil to say a thing like that!* She wrapped the end of Buddy's leash around the hook, and the dog flopped down to watch what she was doing.

It didn't take long to sweep the stable. Neil grabbed a bale of straw and cut the string so that they could spread it across the floor. By the time they'd finished,

Natalie had bits of straw sticking out of her hair. Andi began to suspect that she was on a mission for Grade-A membership in the 4-H Club. She certainly looked the part, although Andi couldn't imagine Mr. and Mrs. Peters being too pleased about having a batch of ducklings swimming in their pool!

"Andi, could you get a rug from the storeroom at the end of the barn?" Neil asked. "I think Badger needs an extra layer. He's our oldest horse, and he really feels the cold."

The storeroom was crammed full, reminding Andi of her closet crossed with an outdoor-supply store. The floor was hidden beneath a stack of buckets, a roll of chicken wire, and a variety of spades, brooms, pitchforks, and other tools that Andi didn't recognize. At the far end, shelves reached from floor to ceiling. They were crowded with pieces of tack, cleaning cloths, grooming brushes, and an assortment of boxes containing whoknew-what. And she thought Buddy needed a lot of accessories!

She searched around, but she couldn't find any rugs. She went back to the stable. "Sorry, Neil, but I can't find it."

He frowned. "It's right on the shelf in front. I don't know how you missed it."

Andi shrugged. She was doing her best. It wasn't *her* fault if things weren't where he thought they should be. "Then find it yourself."

The girls both followed him back as he went to look for the missing rug. He flung open the storeroom door. "It's right here, on the — " The words died on his lips. "Where did it go?"

"I'm off now, Neil. See you tomorrow," said a deep voice.

Andi whirled around. A tall man in his mid-forties, with dark curly hair flecked with gray, was crossing the yard with a rather rusty bike.

"Jed, you haven't seen Badger's rug, have you?" Neil asked.

"No, sorry." Jed climbed on his bike and pedaled away down the drive.

"Who was that?" Natalie asked.

"Jed Rogers, the new stablehand. He started last week — just turned up one day looking for work, which made Mom happy since we're really busy right now."

"So you don't know much about him?" Andi asked, immediately suspicious.

"Not much, I guess. But he's really good with horses."

Andi and Natalie exchanged glances. "Did he bring references from his previous jobs?" Andi asked.

"I don't know. Why?"

"Well, don't you think it's a bit of a coincidence that just after a new stablehand is hired, one of the ponies disappears?"

Neil stared at her. "You don't mean . . . "

"That Jed stole Sunshine? He might have. Did he seem particularly interested in her?" Andi felt shaky inside. They could be really close to catching the thief!

"He likes all the horses. I haven't noticed that he has any special favorites." Neil ran a hand through his hair distractedly. "But lots of stuff's disappeared since Jed's been working here. I thought he was just putting things back in the wrong places, but there's no reason for him to have moved Badger's rug. . . . "

"Maybe he stole it," Andi finished for him. "And maybe he stole Sunshine, too. If he's that good with horses, he'd have been able to make her go with him, even if she was nervous." Her hopes were soaring. Maybe this wasn't going to be such a hard case to solve, after all. "Come on, let's follow him!"

Chapter Eight

"Hang on, Andi," Natalie said. "Jed couldn't have stolen Sunshine. The police must have checked him out already, along with all the other staff at the center."

"Maybe he hid Sunshine really well. You have to admit he looks suspicious."

"I guess . . ."

"Okay, then!" Andi raced after Jed, desperate to keep him in sight, though he was pedaling fast. "We can't let him get away," she called over her shoulder.

"Okay, okay." Natalie ran after her. "But there's no way we'll be able to keep up with him. I know you're a fast runner, Andi, but he's on his bike. You'll never catch him. And if *you* can't do it, *I* won't stand a chance."

"Take my bike. And my mom's," Neil said. "They're over here."

These bikes were far from the mountain bikes they

were used to riding, but Andi wasn't going to let that stop her. "Quick, Nat!" She jumped onto the nearest bike and set off down the drive. "Look after Buddy for me, Neil!" she yelled over her shoulder.

"Sure!" Neil shouted back.

"Wait for me, Andi!" Natalie called.

Andi's legs pumped furiously as she bounced and rattled along the potholed road, but she seemed to be making painfully slow progress. She tried clicking through the gears, but none of them made much differ-ence to her speed. By the time she reached the main road, Jed was a long way ahead and Andi's legs felt ready to drop off. But there was no way she was giving up now. This was their best lead yet!

Natalie drew level with her, red-faced and breathless. "I can't believe we're doing this!" she wheezed.

"Just keep pedaling," Andi panted.

To her relief, the road began to slope downhill. She sat up straighter on the seat and let the bike freewheel. Ahead, she could see a pair of houses at the bend in the road. "I hope he lives in one of those," she said. "I don't want to ride much farther on this bone shaker."

Sure enough, Jed skidded to a halt in front of the first house and went inside, leaving his bike propped against the porch.

"Thank goodness," Natalie said with a groan.

"Let's pull in here," Andi suggested when she and Natalie were about twenty yards from the house. An ivy-covered hedge grew alongside the road, and they pushed the bikes into it to hide them.

"What do we do now?" Natalie hunched over with her hands on her knees, trying to get her breath back.

"Let's look around. Maybe Sunshine's out back."

They walked down the hill with their hands in their pockets, trying to look like hikers out for an afternoon stroll. Andi scanned the windows as they approached the house, but nobody was looking out.

Jed's yard was enclosed by a wooden fence about four feet high. They ducked down when they reached it, then crept along beside it. A gate led into the back. Natalie opened it cautiously, and they tiptoed through into a tangle of weeds and overgrown shrubs.

"He's not too into gardening, by the look of it," Andi whispered. Then she clutched Natalie's arm. A large flat-roofed shed stood at the back of the yard. It was the perfect place to keep a stolen pony!

"Are you sure this is a good idea?" Natalie asked. "I mean, wouldn't the police have already checked this place out?"

"What if they haven't?" Andi pointed out. "They might

have been concentrating on finding the truck Shona saw and not come here at all." She crept forward. "Sunshine could be just a few yards away, Nat."

"Okay," Natalie said. "I guess it would be dumb not to check it out now that we're here."

They tiptoed toward the shed, trying not to get snagged on the bushes. At the very end of the yard, the shrubs had been cleared, leaving a patch of bare mud.

"Yuck!" Natalie said in a low voice.

Slipping and sliding, they picked their way across the mud to the shed. The door was bolted on the outside with a large iron link. "Why would anyone need to lock their shed from the outside?" Andi whispered. "What's he locking *in*?"

Natalie pressed her ear to the door. "I think you're right, Andi!" she gasped. "There is something in there. I can hear it moving around." Her eyes shone with excitement.

Andi listened, too. Something big was bumping around inside.

"Well, it could be Jed's own horse," Natalie whispered.

"I doubt that he's got one," Andi said. "Not if he rides a bike to the stables. No one would choose to ride a bike up that hill if they could let a horse carry them instead. And he could easily leave it in the stable or the paddock all day." She grinned at Natalie. "Looks like the Pet Finders have done it again!"

"Let's get her out!" Natalie seized the bolt and slid it back. As she pushed the door open, they heard a loud squeal. A moment later, an enormous bristly pig came charging out. It was pink and black, with beady eyes and sharp teeth. Natalie screamed and tried to get out of the way, but she slipped in the mud and fell over, arms flailing.

The pig swerved and cannoned into Andi's legs. Andi stumbled back, her arms flapping wildly as she tried in vain to keep her balance. "Look out, Nat!" she screeched as the pig came galloping back, snorting. She struggled to stand up, but the mud was too slippery. Even getting onto her knees was difficult, and all she could do was slither aside every time the pig charged.

Natalie lurched toward her, somehow managing to stay on her feet. She was plastered with mud from head to toe. She held out a filthy hand to Andi. "Let's get out of here."

"What's going on?" bellowed a furious voice suddenly.

Andi slithered around and felt her heart plummet into her very muddy sneakers. Jed was standing at the edge of the muddy space, arms folded, glaring at them. Be-

hind him was an elderly man, wearing slippers and smoking a pipe. He was grinning broadly.

Andi took Natalie's mud-caked hand and struggled to her feet. She looked around warily for the pig. It had stopped charging around and was rubbing its back against the fence on the far side of the pen.

"Well?" Jed demanded, taking a step forward.

Andi couldn't think of a thing to say. They could hardly tell him the truth, that they'd suspected him of stealing Sunshine. She gazed at him blankly, shivering underneath her liberal coating of cold, wet mud.

"I'm sorry," Natalie said. She turned an agonized gaze on Andi, struggling for an explanation. "We're . . . um . . . searching for a lost cat. We thought it might have hidden in your shed. We didn't realize there was a pig inside." She tried to flip her hair back from her face, but it was caked in mud and just stuck to her hand.

"Is that so?" Jed said, clearly not believing a word.

"Looks like they wanted our Bessie," the older man said. "I reckon we should call the police."

Andi gulped. She could just imagine what her mom would say if she had to pick them up from the police station.

"We weren't trying to steal your pig, honestly." Keeping a close eye on the pig, Natalie edged unsteadily toward the shed. She picked up what looked to Andi like a huge lump of mud.

The muddy lump turned out to be Natalie's backpack. She brushed the mud from the fastener, then unbuckled it. With a shaky hand, she took out a flyer for the Pet Finders Club and handed it to Jed. "See? That's us. The Pet Finders Club."

Jed scanned the flyer briefly, then passed it to his father.

"We're looking for a . . . a Russian blue cat," Andi said, remembering a valuable pedigree that they'd tracked down once.

"We've been searching everywhere," Natalie added.

The old man chewed the end of his pipe. "Maybe they're not thieves after all."

"Just what I was thinking," Jed agreed. "Though they could be pretty much anything under all that mud."

"So, can we go, then?" Andi asked, relieved that Jed didn't recognize them from the riding center.

"I guess so. But I wouldn't recommend coming back here. Our Bessie doesn't like being disturbed." Jed stepped aside so they could pass him.

All Andi wanted to do was run out of the yard, jump on Neil's bike, and pedal away as fast as she could, but she and Natalie were ankle-deep in sticky mud. They squelched through it, hot with embarrassment, watched closely by the beady-eyed pig.

At last, they were back on the road. They sped up past the cottage, though their mud-plastered sneakers made their feet heavy and clumsy.

They retrieved their bikes from the hedge. "Thanks for that, Andi. Not!" Natalie said. "You almost got us arrested!"

Andi began to scrape mud off her sneakers with a stick. "I know. Sorry. But it did look suspicious, and . . ." She broke off.

Natalie was grinning at her, her teeth gleaming white in her filthy face. "You look like the creature from the Black Lagoon," she said, starting to laugh.

"So do you."

Suddenly, they both broke into helpless giggles. "We must have looked so ridiculous trying to run away from that pig!" Natalie hooted with laughter.

Andi couldn't stop laughing until she remembered why they'd come here in the first place. Suddenly, her high spirits drained away. "But we still didn't find Sunshine."

Natalie stopped, too. "I know. I guess we'd better get back to the stables."

They scraped off as much mud as they could, then rubbed their hands on the grass to clean them.

"I have a bad feeling about this case," Andi admitted.

Natalie sighed. "Me, too. I thought if we could find small animals like cats and dogs, then finding an animal as big as a pony would be a piece of cake. But it isn't." She ran her fingers through her mud-matted hair.

"The thing is," Andi said, "if cats and dogs wander off, you can be pretty sure they haven't gone far from home. But if Sunshine's been stolen, then she could have been taken anywhere, even clear across America." She hated to admit it, but this was starting to look like one case they just weren't going to solve.

The next day after school, Andi took Buddy for a walk in the park. She'd arranged to meet Natalie and Tristan there, and they were waiting by the entrance. Natalie had Jet, her black Labrador, with her.

"Hi, Andi," Tristan said. "Wow, you clean up nice."

"So, you've heard about our great pig adventure?"

Tristan grinned. "Natalie told me. I wish I'd been there to see it for myself. You could at least have taken some pictures," he teased.

They went into the park and Andi let Buddy off his leash. He went tearing away, then circled back, as though he were a sheepdog and they were his flock. Jet watched him wistfully. "Don't even think about it,"

Natalie said to Jet, who had a habit of running off when he was let off his leash.

"Why don't you take him to dog school?" Andi suggested. "Labradors are usually easy to train."

"That's not a bad idea," said Natalie thoughtfully.

"Any more clues?" Tristan asked as they headed toward the woods.

"Neil said that some things are missing from the stables," Andi told him. "Badger's rug, for a start. And there's a new stablehand. . . . "

"Oh, didn't I tell you?" Natalie cut in. "Neil called me today. He asked Jed about the missing things, but Jed doesn't know anything about them. Neil's sure he didn't take them."

"Well, at least that means we won't have to meet up with his pig again," Andi said.

"Whoa!" Tristan yelled suddenly. He darted away.

"Tristan?" Andi called after him. "Doughnut delivery?" she joked to Natalie.

"No, look!" Natalie grabbed her arm. "It's that truck! It totally fits the description of the one Shona saw the day Sunshine was stolen!"

Andi looked where she was pointing. Sure enough, a green horse truck with a smashed-in fender was driving along the road next to the park!

Chapter Nine

The truck turned left. Tristan came running back to them. "Quick! That road leads around behind the woods. He'll come out on Half Mile Lane. We can cross the middle of the park and cut him off." He took off in the opposite direction.

"Not more running!" Natalie groaned. All the same, she raced after Tristan, with Jet loping beside her.

Andi whistled for Buddy. He was quite a distance away, down by the lake, but he came scampering over, barking with excitement. "Come on, Bud!" Andi sprinted after Natalie and Tristan. Buddy easily kept pace with her, his mouth open in a wide doggy grin. There was nothing Buddy liked better than a good run.

Normally, Andi could outrun Tristan and Natalie easily. Today, to her surprise, it took her a couple of

minutes to catch up with both of them. She passed
Natalie first, who was red-faced and panting hard but
showed no signs of giving up. Tristan was a little way
ahead, running strongly.

Wow! Andi thought. *Being in the Pet Finders Club must
be getting them into shape!*

Pushing herself harder, she caught up with Tristan,
then raced on to the gate. She stooped down and
clipped on Buddy's leash before heading to the side-
walk. "Come on, boy! Let's see if we can find that truck."
There was no sign of it yet — it must still be driving
along the winding road that ran through the trees on
the west side of the park.

Tristan pounded up to join her. Panting hard, he
looked hopefully along the road in both directions. A
few moments later, Natalie arrived with Jet. "Can . . .
you . . . see . . . it?" She gasped for air.

"Not yet," Andi admitted.

Natalie clung to the park railings, trying to get her
breath back.

Suddenly, the green truck appeared at the top of the
hill. "There it is!" Andi exclaimed.

Sensing her excitement, Buddy began to bark.

"Uh, what are we going to do now?" Tristan asked,
looking uncertain.

"We can't just let it drive past," Natalie protested. "This is our best chance of cracking this case."

"What do you suggest? That we all jump out into the road to stop the truck, and then accuse the driver of being a horse thief?" Tristan said scornfully.

"Hang on," Andi said. "It's turning." The truck was slowing down next to a junction. "Where does that road go, Tris?"

His face lit up. "The truck stop! Don't you remember, where we went looking for Apple's owner?" They'd found Apple, an oatmeal-colored terrier, several months earlier in a backyard not far from Andi's house.

"Let's go. Come on, Jet!" Natalie began to jog along the road.

Andi and Tristan sped after her.

They soon reached the truck stop. "Can you see the truck?" Tristan asked.

"There!" Natalie shouted. The green truck was parked between two eighteen-wheelers, its dent with the red scrape of paint clearly visible. The driver was still inside, rummaging through the glove box. As they approached, he snapped it shut and climbed out. He was a stocky man with bushy gray hair.

Andi stepped back hurriedly as the man looked around, and her foot came down on top of Tristan's.

The horse truck driver walked toward the café, whistling.

"Let's check out the truck," Tristan whispered, standing on one leg and rubbing his smashed toes. "Maybe Sunshine's in the back."

Andi's knees were quaking as they crept to the horse truck. She pressed her ear to the door. There was no sound, but perhaps Sunshine was standing still — or lying down, hurt!

Checking first to be sure nobody was watching them, they stole along the side of the truck to the groom's door, just behind the cab. Tristan seized the handle. To Andi's surprise, it wasn't locked. The rusty hinges squealed as they tried to open it, making them all freeze. Surely somebody must have heard that! But nobody came running to ask what they were doing.

They swung the door open.

The floor of the truck was strewn with straw and an empty hay net hung from a ring on the side, but there was no sign of Sunshine.

"She's not here," Andi said, disappointed.

"He must have taken her somewhere else," Natalie groaned. "He has to be the thief. Why else would he have been belting away from the Riding Center on the same day that Sunshine vanished?"

"What do we do now?" Tristan asked.

"I'm going to talk to the driver." Natalie thrust Jet's leash into Tristan's hand and strode away, heading in the direction of the café.

Andi and Tristan ran after her. "Wait!" Andi caught her arm. "What are you going to say?"

Natalie was grim-faced. "I'll think of something."

The driver was talking to another man outside of the café.

"Excuse me," Natalie said, stepping forward. "I couldn't help noticing the horse stickers on the windshield of your truck. Do you know the way to Hollow Creek Riding Center?"

The driver looked around. "I most certainly do. I must have driven past it at least a dozen times last week. I was trying to find a farm in the mountains, and I had to keep turning around. Thought I'd never find it!"

Natalie glanced over her shoulder at Andi and Tristan before going on. "I hear they've got some gorgeous horses there. At Hollow Creek, I mean."

The second driver, a plump man in his early fifties, grinned. "Sounds right up your alley, Mac."

"Oh, do you like horses?" Natalie asked. Andi was amazed at the way she made the question sound so casual. She was glad she didn't have to speak to the driver herself; she probably wouldn't have been able to think of a thing to say.

"Can't stand them," Mac said unexpectedly. "Scared stiff, to tell the truth. I was kicked by a mustang when I was young — broke my arm, it did! I've never been near a horse since."

"But your truck . . . " Natalie began.

"Oh, yeah. Well, I bought it from a stable owner a few months ago, but I just use it for transporting cattle. They're a lot easier to handle, I can tell you! Now about those directions to Hollow Creek . . . " He glanced around and his eyes rested on Andi. "Are you three together?"

"I . . . um . . . " Natalie sputtered.

Too late. Andi realized that she was wearing a Hollow Creek Riding Center T-shirt. The logo was showing, and the truck driver must have noticed it. She pulled her coat across, but the damage was done.

"Look, I don't know what you're up to," he snapped, "but if your friend's got a Hollow Creek shirt already, then I guess she knows the way." He stalked into the café.

Natalie scooted back to Andi and Tristan. "He can't be the thief if he's scared of horses."

"I guess not," Andi agreed. "He'd never be able to get Sunshine into his truck."

"Maybe he was lying," Tristan pointed out. "I mean, he might have told people he was scared of horses so nobody would suspect him when horses started disappearing."

"But what are we going to do?" Andi said. "We can't follow him when he leaves here. He's in a truck. We won't be able to keep up."

"And he's pretty scary," Natalie said. "Did you see the way he looked when he spotted Andi's T-shirt? I'm not sure I'd want to go snooping around *his* farm."

"He's our best lead," Tristan said determinedly. "And I'm not giving up on him just yet. Let's hide near his truck and see what he does when he comes out. Or . . ." His eyes gleamed. "We could hide in the back of his truck and find out where he goes."

"No way!" Andi exclaimed. "That would be way too dangerous!"

"Okay, okay, it was just an idea! But there's no harm in watching what he does."

They headed back toward the truck and hid behind a huge eighteen-wheeler nearby. "Wait here and keep watch," Tristan said.

"Why? What are you going to do?" Natalie asked.

"I'm going to see if his cab's unlocked." Tristan checked all around, then darted to the horse truck.

"Tristan!" Andi called after him. "Come back!"

He tried the door and it swung open.

"It's open." Natalie groaned. "Come on. We'd better go see what he's up to."

She and Andi ran to the truck. Tristan was already inside, peering into the glove compartment. He pulled out a tattered pamphlet and leafed through it. "He was telling the truth," he said with a sigh. "He *does* use his truck for cattle. Look at this." It was a program from a cattle sale. "He's circled some of the cows in here." Tristan pushed the program back where he found it. "It looks like his story's starting to add up."

He jumped down from the cab and shut the door. "Quick!" Natalie whispered hoarsely. "He's coming back!"

They dashed behind the next truck and waited, hearts thumping, until they heard the truck drive away.

"This is hopeless!" Andi said in frustration as they trudged back across the park. "That truck was our only lead, but the driver obviously isn't the thief."

"We just don't have a handle on this case at all," Tristan said gloomily. "And . . . " He was interrupted by Natalie's phone ringing.

She pulled it out of her bag and checked the caller ID. "Hmm, I don't know this number."

"Maybe it's a new case," Andi said, perking up.

"Preferably an easy one," Tristan added. "Like a cat stuck up a tree, surrounded by people pointing at it."

Natalie answered the phone, switching it to speakerphone so they could all hear. "You're looking for a missing pony," said a gruff voice.

"Who is this?" Natalie gasped.

"It doesn't matter. The pony's fine, okay? She doesn't need to be found." The line went dead.

"We just spoke to the thief!" Andi exclaimed.

"It was a disguised voice," Tristan said. "Nobody really speaks like that. You couldn't even tell if it was a man or woman."

Natalie grabbed a pen and a notepad from her bag and jotted down the caller's number. "Weird number! It ends in four eights."

"Try calling back," Andi said eagerly. Then she shivered. "Though I'm not sure I want to speak to whoever it was again. That was really creepy. Maybe we should just tell the police."

"We can't let this go." Natalie punched the redial button, and the line began to ring.

Andi held her breath, waiting for someone to pick up, though she couldn't imagine what they'd say. Natalie hung on for ages, but the phone just rang and rang. In the end, they were cut off automatically. "Why did the thief say the pony doesn't need to be found?" she wondered. "And how did he . . . or she know we were looking for Sunshine?"

"The thief must have seen one of the flyers Nat left and guessed that we'd be involved," Tristan said. "But that was a weird thing to say, that Sunshine doesn't *need* to be found. Of course she does. Her owner wants her back. Even a thief would know that."

"Somebody is just trying to scare us off," Natalie decided, "but obviously doesn't know the Pet Finders very well. One anonymous phone call isn't going to stop us!"

They headed to Tristan's house to talk about what to do next.

Mrs. Saunders beamed at them as they came into the kitchen. "Good timing! I've just baked oatmeal-and-raisin cookies."

They followed her into the kitchen, a homey room with a big square table at one end. "Sit down. Cookies and milk all around?"

"You bet!" Tristan agreed enthusiastically.

Mrs. Saunders frowned when they told her about the phone call. "Whoa. This is getting serious."

"They didn't threaten us or anything, Mrs. Saunders,"

Natalie said. She broke off a piece of cookie and dropped it on the floor for Jet. He stood up, his tail wagging, but Buddy was too quick for him and snatched the piece of cookie before Jet could. Jet flopped down again good-naturedly.

Buddy leaped up at Natalie, clearly hoping for another piece of cookie. He knocked into her hand and her phone went flying.

"Bad Buddy!" Andi scolded. "No more cookie for you." She bent down to pick up the phone, then froze. The redial button must have been pressed as it hit the floor. Andi could hear a voice coming from the phone.

"Yeah? Hello?" a man said impatiently. "Is anyone there?"

"What was the last number you called, Nat?" Andi hissed.

Natalie's eyes widened. "The one ending in four eights!"

Chapter Ten

"H . . . hello?" Andi said into the phone, hardly able to believe that she was talking to the horse thief.

"Hi, there. Can I help you?" the man said. He sounded brisk but quite friendly — not at all like the gruff, scary voice that had called before.

"I . . . I'm calling about the missing horse," Andi faltered.

"A missing horse? Why are you calling a diner about a missing horse?"

"What? You're in a *diner*?"

"Young lady, I am always in this diner. I own this diner, and I spend eighteen hours a day here."

"Oh." Andi thought for a moment. "So this is a pay phone I'm calling?"

"That's right."

"Someone called us from this phone about half an hour ago. Do you know who it was?"

"I'm sorry, I really don't have time for this right now. I have a whole roomful of customers waiting to be served," he explained. "Hang on there, Charlene! That guy wanted salad on the side! Look, I gotta go."

"Wait! Don't hang up! What's the name of your diner?"

"Dixie's." And that was it.

Andi told Natalie and Tristan everything the diner owner had said. "It's called Dixie's," she finished.

"Dixie's Diner?" Mrs. Saunders echoed. "I know where that is. We sold a farmhouse just down the road from there." She got a map and spread it out on the table. "It's on this road here."

"That's not far from Hollow Creek!" Tristan looked hopefully at his mom. "Um . . . how do you feel about getting out of the house, Mom? I mean, you've been cooped up inside baking cookies and . . . "

"Tristan, I am *not* driving you to meet a horse thief! Let's call the police and let them handle it."

"But, Mrs. Saunders, the thief won't still *be* at the diner," Natalie said.

"And we can't call the police unless we have something definite to tell them," Andi added persuasively. "If we go to the diner, maybe we can get a description of the person who used the phone."

"Come on, Mom!" Tristan begged.

Mrs. Saunders sighed. "Okay, I guess. But I'm coming in with you. And if the thief's still there, we're coming right out again. Is that clear?"

"Sure. Thanks, Mom." Tristan drained the last of his milk. "Come on!"

Dixie's Diner was set on a narrow road about three miles from the Hollow Creek Riding Center. It was a square single-story building with a life-size plastic cowboy outside. The name was painted in red letters above the door.

They left Buddy and Jet in the car and hurried inside. "Wow, this place is really *themed*," Natalie whispered in Andi's ear.

Country music was playing loudly, and the waitresses were dressed as cowgirls, complete with Stetsons and cowboy boots. Lassoes and WANTED posters for Wild West outlaws were hung on the walls. A menu was chalked on a blackboard behind the counter. "Mmm, that Wyatt Earp burger with grilled eggplant sounds good," Tristan said.

"We didn't come here to eat," Natalie reminded him sternly.

"I'll be right here," Mrs. Saunders said, taking a table near the door where she'd have a good view of the whole diner. "Maybe I'll have some coffee while you're asking questions."

A door led into the kitchen. It stood open, and they could see a man in a striped apron chopping onions. "Hot dog's almost ready!" he called.

"That's the man I talked to on the phone," Andi said, recognizing his voice. She darted to the counter and waved to attract his attention. To her annoyance, he turned away without noticing.

"Won't keep you a minute, honey," said the woman behind the counter. She set down a mug of coffee in front of one of the customers. "There you go, Hank." She turned to the Pet Finders. "Hi, there. What can I get you?"

"We're trying to find someone who made a call from the pay phone here an hour or so ago," Andi said.

"Sorry, I only started work twenty minutes ago. But Charlene's been here all morning." She raised her voice across the diner: "Charlene, you got visitors!"

Charlene, a young waitress with long red hair tied in a ponytail, came hurrying over, tucking her order pad into the wide pocket on the front of her denim skirt. She looked at them curiously.

"We're trying to find a stolen pony," Tristan explained. "Someone called us about her from your pay phone about an hour ago."

Frowning, Charlene pushed back her hat. "Well, a few people have used the phone today. A couple of guys in a pickup truck, and a man with a flat tire called a garage . . . "

"Did you know any of them?" Andi asked eagerly.

"No. Just passing through, I guess, and thought they'd stop in."

"What did they look like, these men who made the calls?" Natalie prompted.

Charlene frowned. "The pickup truck guys were in their mid-twenties, I'd say. And wearing denim jackets. The other guy had a beard and was a bit overweight."

"Did you hear what they said?" Tristan questioned.

"No chance!" Charlene nodded toward the kitchen. "If Mr. Dixon thought I was standing around listening to phone conversations, he'd have something to say about it."

"So it could have been any one of those three men who called us," Tristan said thoughtfully. They started to head for the door.

"Well, wait," Charlene said, calling them back. "You didn't let me finish. There was a girl, too."

"Did she use the phone?" Andi asked excitedly.

"Yep. But she only made a very short call. I asked her if she needed any help — she looked upset — but she left in a hurry."

"Can you remember what she looked like?" said Tristan.

"Tall for her age, and real thin. She had blond hair, cut real short."

Andi was astonished — that sounded exactly like Sara! Could she have made the call to Natalie? Did that mean *she'd* stolen Sunshine?

The man who'd been chopping onions appeared at the kitchen door. "Charlene, I don't pay you to stand around talking all day!"

Charlene jumped. "I told you! I have to get going," she said. "I hope you find the pony." She quickly began to clear one of the tables.

"But there are other questions we need to ask you," Natalie said.

"No, it's okay," Andi told her. "I know who it is!" She dragged Natalie and Tristan outside. She could hardly believe it. How could Sara be the thief?

"What on earth are you talking about?" Natalie pulled herself free and smoothed down her jacket.

"I recognized the description Charlene gave us." Andi sank down on the low wall surrounding the diner. "It's Sara! You know, the girl who ran away." Shakily, she told them about Sara's weird behavior at the Riding Center.

"She kept looking at Sunshine all the time. And she wanted to ride her, but Shona wouldn't let her."

Tristan sat beside her. "She wouldn't have taken Sunshine just because of that!" He broke off as a man came out of the diner and climbed into a pickup truck. "There has to be some other reason," he finished as the man drove away.

Andi shrugged. "I guess she wasn't thinking straight. Maybe she really wanted a pony of her own, but her parents wouldn't let her have one. Right now, it doesn't matter why she did it, we have to find her before the police do. She's in real trouble, and maybe we can help." She jumped up and looked around, trying to imagine which direction Sara had gone when she left the diner.

"It'd be better if she brought Sunshine back herself," Natalie said, "rather than waiting until she's hunted down by the police."

"We'd better start searching," Tristan said, looking around anxiously. "She can't be far if she was here only an hour ago." He paused and turned to the girls. "Didn't you say her aunt lived on a farm?"

"Halfpenny Farm. It's not far from Andi's house," Natalie told him. "And it's not all that far from here, either, if you're on horseback and can cut across the fields."

"I bet she's there!" Tristan exclaimed. "There are probably a ton of sheds or barns where she could hide. And she might guess her aunt went to help her mom look for her closer to home."

Mrs. Saunders came out of the diner. "That was quick. I didn't even finish my coffee. Did you learn anything?"

"Plenty. We'll tell you in the car," Tristan said. "Right now we need to get back to Orchard Park, quick!"

They scrambled into the car. Buddy jumped in Andi's lap the moment she sat down and began licking her furiously.

Tristan told his mom what they'd found out. "You should really call the police," she said. "This is important. The sooner that poor girl is back home, the better."

"I'll do it," Natalie said.

"Good, let's go." Mrs. Saunders started the engine. She paused with her hands on the steering wheel and met Andi's eyes in the mirror. "Oh, that poor girl," she said, echoing Andi's thoughts. "I hope they find her soon."

Natalie pulled out her cell phone as the car sped away. "Ugh! The battery's dead!"

"Never mind. We'll call from Halfpenny Farm," Andi said. "Then, hopefully, we'll be able to tell the police that we've solved two cases in one."

*   *   *

Sara's uncle, Mr. Walker, came running down the drive-way when Mrs. Saunders's car pulled up. "Oh," he said flatly as the Pet Finders climbed out. "Can I help you? I thought you would be bringing news about my niece."

"We are!" Andi exclaimed. "We think we know where she might be. She's taken a pony from Hollow Creek Riding Center, and we think she's hiding in a building here."

Mr. Walker stared at her. "Taken a pony? Hiding here?"

"We think she called us from a diner near the stables just over an hour ago, so she must be hiding some-where not too far away. This seems like a pretty good place to start looking."

"Come on, then." Mr. Walker led the way to the first barn and threw open the door. The Pet Finders crowded inside, squinting into the gloom. There were a couple of pieces of farm machinery in the shadows, but that was all.

"No sign of her in here," Andi said, disappointed.

They ran to the next barn, and the next, but Sara and Sunshine were nowhere to be found. "I really thought we were on to something," Tristan sighed. "Is there any-where else on the farm where she could hide?"

"Not really." Mr. Walker frowned. "Why would she steal a pony? I know she was upset when Buttercup was stolen, but that was a year ago. It can't be anything to do with that."

"Can we use your phone, please, Mr. Walker?" Natalie asked. "We should tell the police what we found out."

Andi's heart sank. She knew the police had to be told what was going on, but she'd really hoped the Pet Finders would find Sara first.

"Of course." Mr. Walker led the way to the farmhouse. Buddy pressed close against Andi's leg, as though he could sense her disappointment and wanted to cheer her up.

"I don't suppose you've got a photo of Sara that we could borrow, do you, Mr. Walker?" Andi asked as they went inside. "We could show it to the waitress at the diner, just to make sure that it really was Sara who made the call."

"Here you go." Mr. Walker took a photo from the living room mantelpiece and handed it to her. Sara was beaming into the camera beside a well-groomed buckskin pony who wore a big red rosette on her bridle.

Andi glanced at it, then said in astonishment, "This is Sunshine!"

"No, that's Buttercup," Mr. Walker corrected. "Sara's pony that was stolen last summer."

Andi looked at the photo more closely. "This pony

doesn't have a freeze brand, but it is *definitely* Sunshine. Look, you can see the dark stripe in her tail."

Tristan, Natalie, and Mr. Walker looked at her, totally stunned. "So, Sunshine *was* really Sara's stolen pony, Buttercup?" Tristan said. "No wonder she kept staring while you were riding her, Andi! She must have been amazed to find her pony after all this time!"

"But how did Sunshine end up at the O'Connors' riding school?" Andi wondered. "You don't think . . . ?" She trailed off, hardly able to believe the suspicion that was forming in her mind.

"That the O'Connors are horse thieves?" Tristan finished for her in a shocked voice.

Andi shivered. "They can't be," she whispered. But what other explanation was there?

When they left, Mr. Walker was trying to get in touch with Sara's parents to tell them the latest news, which was more hopeful, yet more startling than anything else so far.

"What did the police say, Nat?" Andi asked as the Pet Finders headed to Andi's house.

"They're sending someone to the diner to talk to Charlene." Natalie sighed. "And I guess they'll want to interview the O'Connors, too."

Andi squeezed her arm. Poor Nat! It had been a shock for all of them to discover that the O'Connors had probably stolen Sunshine, but it was worse for Natalie because she was so fond of Neil. "Mrs. O'Connor seemed so nice," she said. "I wonder if any of their other horses are stolen."

"Maybe we're wrong about all this," Tristan suggested as they turned onto Andi's road. "Maybe there are two buckskin ponies with dark stripes in their tails."

"I doubt it," Andi said. It would be a pretty unlikely coincidence for Sara to be involved with two ponies with the same unusual coloring.

"When we get to your house, I'm going to call Neil and ask him where they got Sunshine," Natalie decided.

"Don't tell him about the photo," Andi warned. "We don't want the O'Connors realizing we're on to them. They might hide evidence."

"It's probably too late to worry about that," Tristan pointed out. "I bet the police are there now, questioning them."

Andi's mom was upstairs in her study when they went in. "Hi!" she called.

"Hey, Mom. Is it okay to make a phone call?"

"Sure, honey."

The Pet Finders huddled around the phone. Natalie's

hands were shaking as she dialed the number of the riding stables. Andi squeezed her arm, wishing she could make her friend feel better.

There was a tense pause while they waited for someone to answer the phone.

"Hello, Hollow Creek Riding Center." It was Neil's voice.

"Hi, Neil. This is Natalie." Her voice was squeaky with strain.

"Is there any news? Have you found Sunshine?" He sounded genuinely concerned, but Andi was sure he was acting so they wouldn't suspect anything.

"No, not yet. Listen, we were wondering . . . " Natalie frowned while she figured out what to say. "We were wondering where you got Sunshine. I mean, if she got loose, she might have tried to head back to where she came from."

"Oh, right." He paused. "Hang on, I'm trying to remember."

Andi made a face at Tristan. Neil could be frantically trying to work out a believable story.

"I'm pretty sure we bought her from a dealer right across the state," he continued. "It would be a long way for her to go, and she'd have to cross freeways to get back there, so I hope she hasn't tried it. But it's a good idea. I'll give them a call to see if she's turned up."

Natalie gave Andi and Tristan a thumbs-up. "Good idea. Let us know what you find." She hung up, beaming. "See, I knew Neil wasn't a thief!"

"But what he said doesn't prove anything," Tristan pointed out. "He didn't give us the name of the dealer, did he? He might just be a good liar, Nat."

"No, he's not! You're wrong about him!" Natalie glared at Tristan. "You don't even know him!"

Andi stepped between them. "Look, arguing isn't going to help find Sara and Sunshine. We need to get back to the stables. There's still a chance we could find her before the police do and let her know that everyone's only trying to help. We know she's not too far from the diner, which means they're probably hiding out in the mountains." She glanced out of the window and shivered. Heavy black clouds were building up. "We'll have to hurry. It looks like there's a storm coming. And it'll be dark soon, too."

Mrs. Talbot came running downstairs. "Any news?"

Andi told her about their startling discovery, that Sara, the runaway girl, might have tried to steal back her own pony. "We're going out to the stables again. We think Sara and Sunshine are hiding in the mountains."

"We'd better get a move on," Natalie said. "The bus to Hollow Creek leaves in ten minutes."

Tristan glanced at his watch and groaned. "I didn't realize it was so late. I'm supposed to be at Paws for Thought in twenty minutes. A rep's coming in to talk to Christine about snakes, and I don't want to miss him. You'll have to go without me, but call me if you find anything." He darted out of the front door.

"I'm not sure that you should go back to the stables today," Mrs. Talbot said. "I don't like the look of that sky, and it's getting late. Leave it to the police to find Sara."

"Oh, Mom, we *have* to go. Sara must be so frightened out there all on her own."

"And she might stay hidden if she sees the police," Natalie added. "Maybe she'll come out for us."

Andi could see that her mom was wavering. "Please, Mom!" she begged. "We're really worried about her."

"Okay, then. I'll give you a ride. But promise me you won't do anything silly, Andi."

"I promise." Andi grabbed her coat and dashed out of the house.

Chapter Eleven

By the time they reached Hollow Creek, the sky was as black as night. The clouds were so low they looked as if they were resting on the mountaintops, and the wind was raging.

As they rushed out of the car, Neil came racing across the yard with an armful of halters. Andi blinked. It was so hard to imagine that he was a horse thief!

"Can you give me a hand?" He had to shout to make himself heard above the screech of the wind. "I need to get the horses in!" He didn't seem to be acting like he had anything to hide. Maybe Natalie was right, and he had been telling the truth about the dealer after all.

Andi and Natalie followed him, battling against the ferocious wind every step of the way. The surface of the duck pond was choppy with waves that splashed against the bank. Andi spotted the ducks sheltering under nearby bushes, heads down and tails turned to the wind.

The red-and-white cows stood in a huddle in their open-fronted shelter at the far end of the field. "Should we bring in the cows, too?" Natalie yelled.

"No, they'll be fine! Their coats will give them enough protection!" Neil shouted back.

The horses were clustered around the gate, stamping their hooves nervously. Neil slipped a halter over Scrumpy's head and thrust the lead-rope into Andi's hand. "Do you think you can manage two?"

"Sure," she replied.

Neil caught Chipper and calmed him by stroking his nose and speaking to him in a low voice. He passed Andi the rope, then caught Tilly, Bonnie, and Flash. Natalie took charge of Tilly while Neil led the other two.

As they crossed the field, rain began to fall. By the time they reached the stable, it was like standing under a faucet. Andi's hair was so wet, it was plastered to her head.

"The police have been here," Neil said as they settled the horses into the stables. "They told us Sunshine used to belong to Sara. Poor girl, I can't believe we bought a stolen pony." He hugged Flash. "I don't know what I'd do if somebody took Flash." He paused, then added, "You guys must have thought we were horse thieves!"

Andi gulped, but Natalie answered straight-faced. "Of course not!"

"We gave the dealer's details to the police," Neil continued, "so they'll know we bought her fair and square. So I guess now you want to try to look for Sara and Sunshine on the mountain."

"That's right!" Andi listened to the rain pounding on the roof and the wind screeching around the stable. "We'd better head out before the storm gets any worse."

"I'll come with you," Neil said. "And we'll take the horses. It'll be quicker that way. Andi, you ride Chipper, and Nat, you can take Bonnie. They'll be the calmest in this weather." He frowned. "I wish Mom could come, too, but she's taken Donna to the farrier. She lost a shoe this morning."

While she saddled Chipper, Andi racked her brain, trying to figure out where Sara could be hiding. She'd need shelter in weather like this. Suddenly, an image of the old buildings clustered high on the mountainside popped into her head. "Hollow Creek Farm!" she burst out. "I bet Sara's taken Sunshine there! Shona pointed it out on our trail ride, so Sara definitely knows about it."

Neil looked at her over the stable partition. He paused with his hands resting on Flash's saddle. "You could be right," he agreed. "We'll head up there first —

as long as the road hasn't been washed away by the storm."

Andi gulped. Finding Sunshine was turning out to be much more of an adventure than they were used to!

Neil led the way through the woods with Natalie close behind him on Bonnie. Andi followed on Chipper, who was smaller than Sunshine and not quite so coopera-tive. Andi had to urge him forward all the time to keep up with the others. The reins slipped in her wet hands and her sodden jeans clung uncomfortably to her legs. Rain dripped from the branches overhead, and the wind, singing like a choir of ghosts, whipped strands of wet hair into her face.

"Come on!" Neil called. "We need to cross the river be-fore it gets too high!"

Andi's heart lurched, and she tried not to think about how they were going to get back again.

Flash broke into a trot, and Bonnie and Chipper sped up, too. Chipper stopped at the edge of the trees and sidestepped restlessly. Andi patted his wet neck. "Sorry, boy, but we can't stop now." She tapped his sides with her heels and he started forward again.

The ground dropped into a dry gully immediately out-side the woods, then climbed again, steeper than ever.

Neil turned in his saddle and called back, "Let Chipper take the lead! He'll be able to find the best path!"

Andi slackened the rein, and Chipper picked his way up the slope.

Suddenly, Flash stumbled on a loose stone. He lurched to one side, sending Neil toppling out of the saddle. He hit the ground hard.

"Neil!" Natalie screamed, leaping off Bonnie.

Andi jumped down from Chipper's back. Keeping a tight hold on his reins, she ran forward, her heart hammering. Neil was hunched over on the ground. His face was very pale and he was biting his lip in agony. Andi caught Flash's reins, then kneeled beside him. "Are you all right?"

"I . . . I guess so."

Natalie gripped Neil's arm. "Aagh! Let go!" he cried as she tried to help him up. "I think I broke my collarbone." He clutched his shoulder, looking whiter than ever.

"What are we going to do?" Natalie looked petrified. "You can't ride like this."

"Leave me here," Neil said. "You have to keep going. If the river floods, Sara could be trapped!"

Andi thought hard. They couldn't leave Neil out in the open, but they didn't have time to take him all the way back to the stables. Suddenly, she remembered the boulder where the snake had frightened Sunshine. "The rock!" she yelled, raising her voice as a gust of wind swept her words away. "You can take shelter there!"

"Right." Catching Andi's hand, Neil hauled himself, slowly and painfully, to his feet. He rested for a moment, leaning on Flash and waiting for the pain to subside. "Okay, let's go."

They settled Neil on the sheltered side of the boulder. He leaned back and shut his eyes, his face pale. "Take Flash for Sara to ride. Sunshine might not be up to carrying her if she's been living rough for a few days. Now get going. Good luck!" He tried to smile encouragingly at them, but his mouth was twisted with pain.

Andi and Natalie climbed onto the horses and set off again. Andi rode in front, leading Flash beside her and trying to remember where the shallow river crossing was. Night was coming, and the light was fading fast now.

"Look!" Natalie shouted, pointing up the mountain.

Shielding her eyes, Andi peered into the rain. She could just make out the ruined buildings high above them. A light glimmered for a moment against one of the dark shapes, and then went out. *It was probably just lightning reflecting off a window*, Andi told herself. *But it could have been the beam of a flashlight. . . .*

Soon they could hear the river, though they couldn't see it in the increasing darkness. Andi took a flashlight out of her saddlebag and shined it ahead. The thin yellow beam lit up the water rushing by, gray and swirling as it broke over jutting rocks.

"We'll never get across!" Natalie shouted.

"It's shallower farther along."

They turned left and rode beside the river. At last, it widened, and the current slowed. Andi halted Chipper and shined the light down into the water. She could see the bottom quite clearly. "There! That's where we cross."

She urged Chipper forward until he was right at the water's edge, placing a hand on his neck to calm him. "I'll go across first." Andi handed Flash's reins to Natalie, then rode into the water. It swirled and splashed around Chipper's hooves, but the current wasn't strong enough to cause him any problems. In a few seconds Andi was on the far bank.

She turned and shined the flashlight out over the water. "It's okay, Nat."

Natalie rode into the beam of light, leading Flash. The water surged around the horses' legs, but they kept going and scrambled out on the bank.

They climbed the grassy slope next, their shoulders

hunched against the rain. "How much farther?" Natalie groaned. "We've been riding for ages."

At last they reached the steep, narrow road that led up to Hollow Creek Farm. It was deeply rutted and covered with shards of loose rock.

The beam of Andi's flashlight was just strong enough to pick out the steep cliff where the farm buildings perched precariously close to the edge. "We're almost there!"

They started up the road, but the horses' feet kept sliding on the loose stones. Chipper whinnied with fear. "It's okay, boy!" Andi patted his neck. "You're doing fine."

The pony took another hesitant step and slid again. Andi looked over her shoulder. Bonnie was struggling, too. "Maybe we should walk up this part." She dismounted, then led Chipper uphill. Without her weight on his back, the pony was more surefooted, and they were soon at the top.

Andi waited while Natalie brought Bonnie and Flash up the steep slope, then they made their way to the gate that led into the yard. It hung open on one hinge, its bottom rail resting on the ground.

"We made it!" Andi said, gazing up at the old clapboard farmhouse. Rain streamed off the girls, and somewhere a barn door crashed in the wind.

Suddenly, the light flashed again, shining from the doorway of an old cattle shed. It wasn't lightning. There was someone here!

"Hold Chipper, Nat!" Andi said excitedly.

She ran across the muddy yard to the cowshed and hesitated at the door. The shadows inside looked deep and frightening, and she remembered Shona saying the old farm looked haunted. *If Sara's in there, she needs our help*, Andi told herself sternly. Mustering all her courage, she stepped inside, her feet crunching over broken tiles.

The cattle shed was divided into two stalls. Andi peered around the partitions, hardly daring to breathe. A pale-looking figure in the second stall was huddled against the wooden partition with her knees pulled up to her chin. She was wrapped in a horse blanket, but she still looked frozen. Sunshine stood beside her, draped in another rug.

"Sara!"

Sara jumped up, startled. She looked terrified and ready to take off right into the storm.

"Wait!" said Andi, holding out both hands. "It's me, Andi. We met on the trail ride, remember? I've come to get you. Everyone's really worried about you."

Tears welled up in Sara's eyes, but she brushed

them away impatiently. "I'm not coming. I'm staying here."

"You can't. It's freezing."

"I don't care!"

Andi thought desperately. She had to persuade Sara to trust her — and fast, before the river got too deep for them to cross. "Look, I know Sunshine's really your pony, Buttercup."

Sara frowned. "How do you know? Nobody knows except me. I told my mom and dad I found her, but they didn't believe me," she said bitterly. She ran her fingers through Sunshine's mane; they were shaking violently, Andi noticed. "I had to get her back. I had to!"

Andi's head was whirling. Sara was clearly determined not to be parted from Sunshine again, but the O'Connors had bought her fairly from the dealer, just like Neil had said. Maybe they'd get to keep her now, not Sara. It was such a mess!

Andi shook her head. Whatever was going to happen, there was no way Sara could stay here. "You can't keep a pony in a place like this, Sara," she said. "I'm no horse expert, but even I know they need proper stabling and care."

"We won't be here much longer." Sara ran her hands down the pony's shoulder, pulling the rug tighter across

her chest. "Buttercup stepped on a stone and went lame, but she'll be better in a couple of days. Then I'm going to take her home and prove to my parents that she really *is* Buttercup. The O'Connors may have branded her, but I've got enough photos to show that she's mine. And I've got blankets and food for her that I took from the stables. She'll be fine until then."

Andi bit back the anger that threatened to burst out of her. Couldn't Sara see the trouble she was in? "Is she still lame?" she asked. They'd never be able to get a lame pony down the steep, stony road.

"I can't ride her yet, but she can walk okay. She'll be better in a couple of days." Sara caught Andi's arm. "Please don't tell anyone where we are. Please!"

"You have to come back with us, Sara. The O'Connors didn't steal Buttercup, I promise. They're really upset that she was stolen. They bought her from a dealer who could have been involved with the horse thieves who took her from you." Andi broke off. She couldn't tell Sara everything would be all right, because there was no way of knowing how this would end. But the police were probably heading up here right now. It would look a lot better for Sara if she came back on her own.

Sunshine whinnied softly, and Andi went over to lay

her hand against the horse's neck. Her skin felt damp and icy, and she was shivering.

"Poor girl," Andi said. "She's not happy here, Sara. Look at her, she's cold and wet. You've got to do what's best for her."

"I am! It's best for her to be with me!"

"But not here." Andi swung the flashlight around, sending the beam over the rubble-strewn floor. "Not in a place like this. Why did you choose to hide here?"

"Because nobody ever comes here. Except you!"

"Look around you," Andi said. "This is no place for a pony. And the rain's getting worse. What if the buildings get washed away altogether?"

Sara gazed around, her face pale and shocked, as though she were seeing her surroundings for the first time. She patted Sunshine's neck. "I'm sorry, girl."

A halter was hanging on the partition. Andi slipped it over Sunshine's head. "Come on. Let's go." She led Sunshine toward the door. For a moment, Sara stayed where she was, her eyes glistening with unshed tears. Then she followed.

Natalie was waiting outside, sheltering under a roof overhang. "Is everything okay?" she asked.

"Yes, Sara's coming back with us."

"Only for Buttercup's sake," Sara added quickly.

It was a brave thing to do, Andi thought, because Sara was going to be in a lot of trouble when they got back. She must love Buttercup very much.

"We've brought Neil's horse, Flash, for you to ride," Natalie told her. "But you'll have to walk down to the end of the road. It's too steep for riding."

Shining the flashlight ahead, Andi led the way down the track. Water cascaded around her feet, snaking between the rocks. Even the horses found it hard going, moving timidly over the slippery surface with their ears flat back and their quarters hunched.

When they were halfway down, lightning fizzed across the sky, casting the mountainside in silver light. The horses neighed and shied at the end of their reins.

"Don't let them go!" Andi yelled. Throwing down the flashlight, she fought to hold on to Chipper, her feet sliding beneath her. The pony plunged wildly, snorting with fear as his hooves sent stones rattling down the slope.

"It's okay, boy! There's nothing to be frightened of." Andi's heart was pounding, but she managed to speak calmly. To her relief, Chipper stopped pulling and stood still. "Good boy." She patted him, trying to reassure him.

"Are you okay to keep going?" When the others nodded, Andi looked around for the flashlight. It had rolled into a water-filled gully but, amazingly, it was still working. Andi splashed over to pick it up.

A few yards farther, the track leveled out and Natalie drew alongside Andi with Bonnie and Flash. "This is so different from the other lost pets we've found," she said miserably. "Usually everyone's happy, but this just feels horrible."

"I know. I keep wondering what's going to happen to Sara and Sunshine." They reached the grass and Andi turned to call back to Sara. "We can ride from here!" The girl nodded, her face almost white in the shadows, and led Sunshine forward to take Flash from Natalie. She swung herself wordlessly into the saddle and looped Sunshine's reins over the pommel.

Keeping close together, they headed down the slope to the river. Andi wished they could speed up, but it would be dangerous to go too fast in the dark.

"It's a lot deeper than when we crossed before," Natalie said anxiously, peering down at the river.

"The current's faster, too," Andi added. The water raced along below Chipper's hooves, frothing against the banks. She stared at the rushing water in dismay. It hardly looked safe to cross, but what choice did they have? They couldn't spend the night outdoors in this torrential rain. What on earth would they do now?

Chapter Twelve

Chipper snatched at the reins and took a step forward.

"What's he doing?" Natalie almost screamed.

Andi tried to gather up the reins and make him stand still. "Whoa, boy!" she called.

Chipper snorted and scraped at the pebbles under his feet. One or two slipped away and vanished into the churning black water.

"Wait!" said Sara, leaning forward in her saddle. "If he thinks it's safe to cross, you have to trust him! Sit still, keep your reins slack, and see what he does."

Andi swallowed hard. She knew Sara was a very experienced rider, but did she know Chipper well enough to trust his judgment about the river? She caught Natalie's eye, and her friend shrugged. There wasn't anyone else around to help them. Taking a deep breath, Andi dropped her hands and let the reins go slack.

With a snort, Chipper put his head down close to the water. Then he dashed into the river and bounded across in three swift strides. Andi gasped and buried her hands in his mane.

"Hold on, Andi!" Natalie shrieked.

But Chipper had already reached the other side and was scrambling out onto the bank.

"We made it!" Andi untangled her fingers from the wiry mane, weak with relief, then turned Chipper so she could shine the flashlight onto the water. "Come on! It's okay to cross."

Bonnie cantered through the river next, with Natalie clinging on, but Sunshine balked, pulling the rein taut against Flash's saddle. Sara leaned over and ran her hand down the mare's neck. "It's okay, girl," she soothed. "You'll be safe with me." Sunshine looked up at her, her eyes rolling, then lowered her head with a shudder of fear.

Andi watched anxiously. Sunshine was frail and exhausted after her time in the run-down cowshed. She hoped Sara could coax her into the water. They simply had to cross quickly before the river got any deeper.

"Come on, girl!" Sara said. "Do it for me!"

Sunshine whinnied, then took a step closer to Flash. Sara straightened up and urged the palomino into the water, twisting in the saddle to check that Sunshine was following. The two horses splashed across, then, half-trotting, half-cantering, joined Chipper and Bonnie on the lower bank.

"Well, that proves it," Andi said to Natalie. "Sunshine *must* be Buttercup. She was so frightened, but Sara calmed her down."

"I know," Natalie agreed. "They've got a real bond." She looked around. "Now we have to find Neil. Can you remember the way to that boulder, Andi?"

"I think so."

They rode downhill for a little way, then Andi gave a triumphant shout. "There!" The beam of her flashlight was trembling across the giant rock.

"Natalie, Andi, is that you?" called a voice from the other side. "Did you find them?"

"Yes," Natalie replied. "They're here!"

Neil struggled to his feet as they rode up to him. He was still very pale and every movement made him wince.

"I'm really sorry . . . " Sara began through chattering teeth.

"Don't apologize now," Neil interrupted. "What about Sunshine? Is she okay?"

"She bruised her frog on a stone, but she's getting better."

Andi guessed that a frog must be part of a horse's hoof. She didn't think Sunshine had adopted any amphibians up at the farm!

Natalie jumped down from Bonnie's back. "I'll give you a boost up onto Andi's horse." She helped Neil to climb up behind Andi.

"Thanks for coming back for me," he said, slipping one arm around Andi's waist so he wouldn't fall off. "I didn't feel like spending . . . " He broke off suddenly. "What's that?" Wobbling beams of light flashed back and forth below them, at the edge of the pinewoods.

"Neil! Andi! Natalie! Where are you?" a man's voice shouted.

"We're here!" Andi yelled back.

The lights turned in their direction.

"It must be the police," Natalie said.

There were six people in the rescue party. They were dressed in neon orange jackets and they carried ropes and powerful flashlights. One of them had a first-aid kit slung on his back.

"What do you kids think you're doing?" demanded one of the officers. "I couldn't believe it when Mrs.

O'Connor called to say she thought you'd gone up the mountain! Didn't you notice the weather?"

Before anyone could reply, there was a great roar from farther up the mountain. "What's that?" Sara screamed.

Every flashlight turned uphill, and Andi saw a great torrent of foaming, bubbling water surging toward them, sweeping rocks and fallen branches ahead of it.

"The river's flooded!" Neil yelled. "Run!"

Everyone glanced around frantically for a moment, wondering which way would be the safest.

"We'll be safe in the woods!" a police officer shouted. "There's a gully that will carry the water away before it reaches the trees." He raced down the hill, beckoning for the others to follow him.

Andi clapped her heels against Chipper's sides and galloped down the hill, trying to block out the sound of the floodwater roaring behind her. If it caught them, they'd be swept away and could be badly injured. And what about Sunshine? She might not be able to outrun the surging water. Neil clung tightly to Andi's waist, his breath coming in painful gasps.

The ponies leaped down into the gully and up the other side, plunging into the trees where the shadows swallowed them up as if someone had just switched off

the light. The riders had overtaken the police officers in their mad gallop, but the men were not far behind now, scrambling up the slope to the trees. The water growled behind them like a bear.

"Come on!" Andi yelled, wheeling Chipper around to watch. To her relief, Sunshine was with them, standing with her head resting on Sara's leg.

The last police officer made it to the top of the gully just as the river poured in behind him, churning and splashing at his heels. There was one dreadful moment when Andi thought the gully might not be deep enough, but then the water level fell back as it poured away down the mountain. She let out a long, shaky breath and relaxed her grip on Chipper's reins.

"It's okay, Andi," Neil said quietly. "We made it. Let's go home."

Andi was sitting by the fire in the O'Connors' house, wrapped in a blanket and warming her hands on a mug of hot chocolate, when she heard her mom arrive. She glanced anxiously at Natalie. "We're going to be in so much trouble."

Mrs. Talbot appeared in the living room doorway, wearing a raincoat, her hair plastered to her head. "Andi, Natalie, thank goodness you're all right!" She ran over and hugged Andi fiercely. "What were you thinking going up the mountain in this weather?" she demanded.

"We found them, Mom — Sara and Sunshine!" Andi looked at Sara over her mom's shoulder, but the girl was staring unhappily into the fire and didn't notice.

"And?" Mrs. Talbot straightened up, and now Andi could see the tension in her face. "You promised me that you wouldn't do anything irresponsible. What if that flood had swept you away?"

"But it didn't, Mrs. Talbot. We're all fine," Natalie said.

"And I promise we won't do anything like that again," Andi said quietly. She hated the fact that she'd made her mom so worried, and she knew how lucky they were that they hadn't gotten seriously hurt.

To Andi's relief, the living room door opened before her mom could say anything else. Mrs. O'Connor came in. "Dr. Richards is here, Neil. He's waiting in your bedroom to check you over."

"Right." Neil stood up, wincing, and followed her out.

"Good luck," Natalie called after him.

The doorbell rang again. "Can somebody get that, please?" Mrs. O'Connor called.

"I will," Andi offered, glad of something to do to break the tension in the room. She knew her mom was still livid about the danger she and Natalie had put themselves in. She wrapped her blanket tightly around herself and hurried to the door.

A woman dressed in rain gear stood there. "I'm Jane Bradley, the veterinarian. Mrs. O'Connor called me to check up on some ponies that were out in the storm."

Sara came running out of the living room. "I'll show you where they are. One of them, Buttercup, is lame. Can you look at her first, please?"

"Sure."

Sara threw off her blanket, grabbed her sodden coat, and raced out into the rain. Andi watched from the door as they disappeared into Sunshine's stable. She wished she knew what was going to happen. Sara would be heartbroken if she had to leave her pony here. And on top of whatever happened to Sunshine, Sara was still in big trouble for taking her in the first place. The police had gone back to report to a more senior officer, but Andi wondered if they'd be back later to arrest her. She couldn't bear to think of Sara locked up!

The doctor, a smiling gray-haired man, came out of Neil's bedroom with Mrs. O'Connor. "Nothing to worry about, Mrs. O'Connor, though he'll be pretty sore for a couple of weeks."

Neil's mom looked very relieved. "Thanks for coming,

Doctor." She held the door for him, then hurried out to speak to the veterinarian.

Andi went back into the living room, suddenly feeling in need of some company. Neil had made it carefully back to his chair and was telling Natalie what the doctor had said. He'd broken his collarbone, but he didn't need to go to the hospital to have it set, luckily.

Andi flopped down on the sofa next to her mom.

"You okay, honey?" Mrs. Talbot asked.

"I guess." It was hard to think that this was yet another successful end to a Pet Finders case. They'd found Sunshine, but they'd opened a whole can of ugly worms at the same time.

A few minutes later, Mrs. O'Connor and Sara came in, shaking raindrops from their hair.

"The horses are fine," Mrs. O'Connor announced. "Even Sunshine. I mean, Buttercup . . . " She broke off as they all heard a car drive into the yard. Mrs. O'Connor turned to Sara. "This should be your parents now, I think."

Sara bit her lip and looked down at her hands. Andi felt a pang of sympathy for her. However much trouble Andi was in with her mom, it was nothing compared with how Sara's parents must be feeling right now. She heard the front door open, then a man spoke. "I'm Mr. Morling, Sara's father. Is Sara here?"

"Yes. Come in." The phone began to ring. "I'm going to grab that," Mrs. O'Connor said. "Go right in."

Sara sat up straighter in her chair, staring at the door.

A tall, fair-haired man appeared in the doorway, with an anxious-looking woman right behind him. Mrs. Walker was there, too, smiling with relief. "Sara!"

Sara stood up and ran into her parents' arms. "We've been so worried about you!" her mom said, smoothing her hair.

Sara pulled away from them and wiped her eyes on her sleeve. To Andi's surprise, she was looking stubborn rather than apologetic. "I'm sorry you've been worried, but I'm not sorry I took Buttercup. She's *my* pony! She should be with me!" Her shoulders slumped. "But I guess there's no chance of that now."

There was a tense silence. Andi glanced at Neil, wondering if he was going to point out that his mom had bought Sunshine fairly and that she belonged to them now. But she saw that Neil's eyes were full of sympathy as he looked at Sara.

Mrs. O'Connor came in. "The police have agreed not to press charges. I told them it wasn't necessary. You shouldn't have taken Sunshine, Sara, but there's no point dwelling on that now."

"What?" Sara was stunned and blinked back tears for a moment before she could respond. "Thank you, Mrs. O'Connor," she said in a small voice. But then, as if thinking that criminal charges were the least of her worries, she looked back at Mrs. O'Connor. "But, what's going to happen to Buttercup?"

Mrs. O'Connor smiled. "Buttercup *is* your pony. I never would have bought her if I'd known that. Our insurance policy will probably cover the money we've lost. Oh, and the police said that the dealer who sold her to us was arrested a few weeks ago. He's in custody somewhere on the other side of the state."

"Do you mean it?" Sara asked, grinning so widely that her whole face was one big smile. "Really? I can have Buttercup back?"

"Of course you can."

A great wave of happiness swept over Andi. Everything was going to be all right! The Pet Finders wouldn't have to be sorry they'd found this missing pet after all! She exchanged a triumphant grin with Natalie. "This was definitely our hardest case yet, Nat."

"Thank goodness it turned out all right," Natalie

replied. "You can always rely on the Pet Finders to find one thing — drama!"

Andi laughed, feeling suddenly light-headed but full of energy, as if she could run ten miles and still have enough strength for a thousand sit-ups.

Mrs. Talbot stood up. "It's time we got home," she said, with a sympathetic glance at Sara's family reunion on the other side of the room. Andi and Natalie followed her to the door. "I'm in for it when I get home," Andi whispered. "My mom couldn't say much in front of all these people, but I know that look she was giving me. She's really going to let me have it."

"See you next Saturday, Andi!" Neil called from the armchair. "I'll try to make sure there are no floods, missing ponies, or runaways to get in the way this time."

For a moment, Andi didn't know what he meant. Then she remembered she still had the rest of her riding lessons at Hollow Creek Riding Center. She bet her dad would be amazed to hear what his present had led to! She pretended to frown for a moment. "That sounds a little boring." Then she grinned at Neil. "I can't wait!"